Walter Raymond

Charity Chance

Walter Raymond

Charity Chance

ISBN/EAN: 9783337045340

Printed in Europe, USA, Canada, Australia, Japan

Cover: Foto ©Andreas Hilbeck / pixelio.de

More available books at **www.hansebooks.com**

BY

WALTER RAYMOND

AUTHOR OF

"GENTLEMAN UPCOTT'S DAUGHTER," "LOVE AND
QUIET LIFE," "TRYPHENA IN LOVE," ETC.

NEW YORK

DODD, MEAD AND COMPANY

1896

University Press:
JOHN WILSON AND SON, CAMBRIDGE, U.S.A.

CONTENTS.

Charity Chance.

CHAPTER I.

BABBLECOMBE.

To see at a glance the little hamlet of
Babblecombe you must stand upon the crest
of the hill.

There in the coombe below, its half-a-
dozen houses, thatched and whitewashed,
snugly lie together close, like eggs of a
greenfinch in a nest of twigs and moss.
The road which wanders winding down the
hill runs straight in front. The woods,
which upon one side cover the steep, reach
down to the slanting gardens at the back.
The brook is so small and overgrown with
bushes, you would never know it was there
but for a gleam of silver where it feeds the
mill.

You can hear the humming of the wheel,
the shiver of the leaves when the wind
sweeps up the coombe, the startled chatter
of the jay as the village boys run through
the wood. But to every sense of rural
sweetness and every charm of sylvan sound
another joy is added. The breath which
sets the gentle ash a-whispering to the
sturdy oak blows fresh with the fragrance
of the brine; and a mile away, a rich gem
set in the open gap between the cliffs,
stretches the broad sea, sometimes deep as
sapphire and sometimes delicate as pearl.
There also are the grey roofs and square
church-tower of the little town of Babblemouth, and the slanting masts of one Cardiff
collier, as at low water she lies in the
square stone harbour upon her side at rest.

Beyond the nest of cottages, but a little
higher on the hillside, a small mansion
stands apart. Whatever the essential feat-
ure which constitutes a house a mansion, —
whether a winding staircase with an oaken
balustrade, a yew hedge, stables with a
weather-cock, or two gates and a carriage-

drive, — this dwelling possesses it above cavil or dispute. A large pillared portico amply supports that dignity, together with the projecting bedroom overhead. At first sight this stately adornment conveys an impression that the house is mostly hall. Yet it is homely, too; for clematis climbs over the front, and a white rose reaches far above the windows. The mansion faces full toward the sea.

Great steamships of Bristol and the Welsh ports pant to and fro in the dim distance; and sometimes, when spring tides run strong, creep up the channel under the cliffs. At summer noon the sunlight gleams on passing sails as white as snow. At eve some weather-beaten brig or schooner, beating west, stands like a blot upon the glory of the setting sun. They pass the place unheeding, their names and destinies unknown. None but the Cardiff collier ever comes to Babblemouth.

The tourist has not found this haven of rest. The cyclist dare not risk the hill leading down to Babblecombe. An atmos-

phere of old-world respectability pervades
everything, from the smoke, domestic, grey
and clean of commerce, which mantles the
town in mist, to the sweet shadow above
the open cottage door between the honey-
suckle and the eaves.

The coombe is a little heaven upon earth,
where everything you say will be repeated,
and everything you do is known.

CHAPTER II.

THE GARDEN PARTY.

"CHARITY, just give me your arm, dear. How warm the sun is! I will sit in the shade by the yew hedge, and they must come to me there. I hope the strawberries will be enough."

"More than enough, dear aunt, you may rest assured," said the girl, tenderly. Then she added, with sudden impatience, "Enough to have satisfied the children of Israel in the wilderness."

Leaning upon her silver-headed ebony stick, but firmly grasping the girl's wrist with a thin hand, half hidden by a lace mitten, Miss Graham cautiously descended the two steps where the French window opens upon the lawn, and they slowly walked along the path together, — Charity Chance and this little lady whom she called "aunt."

They were both beautiful, — Charity in the glorious wealth of her young woman-hood, with everything to learn, and all to live, and before her the broad land of love untrodden and unexplored; and the little cripple, crooked and misshapen from her birth, who had hobbled threescore years alone, brightening every step with the light of her own soul.

By the border where pinks and mignon-ette were in full flower, the woman's fingers pressed more closely upon the girl's arm, and without a word they stopped.

"Stand where I can see you, child," she said, withdrawing her hand and pointing before her with a gesture half playful, half peremptory.

The girl stepped a few paces aside, and, laughing, stood to be looked at. Behind her the grey stones of the house peered between the delicate tracery of a Virginia creeper. At her feet were the flowers.

"Oh, yes, it is all right," she cried, a gleam of mischief flashing in her eyes. "And if not, what matter?"

"Yes," nodded the little lady, with slow deliberation, — "yes, I like you in white. Turn round a little, dear. Yes — and I like you in the hat. It suits you well."

Her mind at rest upon these matters, the striking beauty of the girl forced itself upon her heart afresh.

"Charity! You might be a princess, child," she burst out, in sudden enthusiasm; then she sighed. "But you know the wish of my life, dear. You know the one wish of my life."

A rapid glance of understanding, and the light faded from the girl's face. Her large brown eyes became thoughtful, and she turned away and looked toward the hillside.

It was midsummer. The sky was clear, the air full of light, and sunshine rested upon hill and cliff. Only, far across the sea, a rising cloud, capped with gold, loomed through the grey haze. The woods were still as if asleep; the birds silent, as they often are in the heat of a summer afternoon.   Nature was in suspense.

Charity stood as in a picture, without word or sign of answer, — a girl of nineteen years, tall and shapely as a lily, her frock of white nun's veiling clinging around her shoulders, and falling soft as snow upon her bosom.   The broad Leghorn hat cast a soft shadow across her cheek, but could not altogether keep the sunlight from the red-brown hair that hung in waves upon her forehead.

Her aunt's appeal, pathetic in the love which prompted it, touched no new note. The hope, that could almost bring tears into the little lady's eyes, had been familiar for many a day.   It could not startle; but the heightened colour on the girl's cheek and her quickened breathing betrayed the agitation it had power to arouse.

"Well, well, child.   Come along."   A sigh — an impatient beckoning of the long thin fingers — and side by side, as before, they walked along the path.

The yew hedge beginning by a corner of the house reached the whole length of the lawn. Beside it garden-seats and chairs had been brought in readiness into the shade. To the largest of these, an arm-chair with a high back of carved oak, raised with a cushion and provided with a foot-stool, Miss Graham solemnly ascended, and seated herself in state. By this device, at which some people smiled, the poor little lady sought to cover the unkindness of Nature by concealing her deficiency of stature. In her left hand she still held the silver-headed stick.

Her manner of dress she had not varied for many years.

A soft black satin gown open at the throat; an embroidered muslin kerchief, crossed and fastened with a miniature in an oval frame of twisted gold, — the portrait of a woman, young and beautiful, with feat-ures and expression strikingly like her own; a mushroom hat of plain black straw tied with black ribbons underneath the chin.

The quaintness of this unpretentious

attire was in keeping with the sweet simplicity of the face, which smiled upon
Charity with the unchanging serenity of a
Madonna in the full contentment of mater-
nity. Her forehead was broad and smooth,
with fewer wrinkles than her years might
claim. Her hair, once fair, was not yet
white; and out of her frank grey eyes looked
a soul, alert and happy in the confidence
that it could see nothing but good.

The girl's arm, taken for support, was
still retained from affection.

"Listen, Charity, dear! What is that?"
she suddenly cried, in alarm.

From across the sea, like a warning murmur of discontent, came the sound of distant thunder, and they saw that the cloud
on the horizon had risen rapidly.

"It is a long way off. They have it in
Wales," laughed the girl, in consolation.

"If it should rain — "

The little lady stopped abruptly, and
raised her hands in horror at the thought.
"But somebody is coming, child. I can
hear wheels on the road, and John Sprake

is hurrying to open his gates. Perhaps the Babblemouth people and Graham. Run down to the door, dear, and bring them round here."

As Charity passed along the path, a look of joy and exultation, such as belongs only to a dream of love, flitted across the cripple's face.

Through the gates of Babblecombe House, now open wide, trotted a one-horsed waggonette, bringing the first arrivals to Miss Graham's garden party. But not the Babblemouth people and Graham. Merely the Rev. Mr. Mortimer, rector of Babblemouth, round-faced and clean-shaven, with his tall, lean wife, and a judicious selection from his numerous daughters.

"Put him where he won't get kicked, John," cried he, throwing the reins upon the back of the most patient beast in Christendom.

Then he greeted Charity with condescension. "Oh! How do you do, Miss Chance?" he asked, almost as if her presence were a surprise.

"In the garden, dear, I suppose," piped Mrs. Mortimer, with that rich smile which creams upon the countenance when the milk of human kindness has turned a little sour. She pecked the girl's cheek with her sharp face, and marched away as if she were at home.

"Good afternoon, Charity," said Theodosia, the eldest.

"Good afternoon," echoed Amy and Amelia.

They were shy of Charity Chance, perhaps a little afraid of her.

Tall and straight, and cool even in that hot weather, they shouldered their tennis rackets, and followed their father up the garden path, like grenadiers in single file.

"Amazons!" muttered the girl, contemptuously, between her teeth, "who never read a line in their lives."

And now the guests flocked in apace. Carriages came crawling down the hill, or whisking along the level road from the town, until they were packed in the little courtyard by the stable close as mere carts at a fair. The lawn was crowded with people; lovers already wandered in the laurel labyrinth by the foot of the wood. It would seem that everybody of distinction in the neighbourhood was there, — colonels of militia, captains of volunteers with their ladies, even a Colonial bishop in gaiters, stooping to play at bowls. Everybody either great or impressive — and yet little Miss Graham's face became anxious as she glanced again toward the gate.

At last there dashed up to the portico a splendid landau drawn by a pair of bays and bearing on the panel a shield the size of a dinner-plate. Its blazonry had often awakened the curiosity and excited the admiration of Babblemouth. It was understood to be quarterly: 1st and 4th az., 3 stags passant ar. for Poltimore, 2nd and 3rd sa., 3 ducks plucked and trussed, or beaked, legged and skewered gules for Briggs. As Mr. Poltimore-Briggs slowly descended and assisted his second wife (the first had been merely Mrs. Poltimore, and passed away before he had assumed the arms and dignity of Briggs) to alight, many an eye was turned to look at them. Even the bishop himself stood erect, the bowl poised upon his ten fingers, and suffered a grave smile to suffuse his classic face.

For Mr. Poltimore-Briggs was a man of the finest presence. Six feet tall at least, and proportionately portly and important. And he wore a spacious waistcoat of snowy white, and a long, old-fashioned gold chain around his neck, and a broad blue necktie, with white spots on it, tied in a bow, and shepherd's plaid trousers and spats, and the blandest expression that ever veiled a mortal face. He closely followed Mrs. Poltimore-Briggs, who was small, sharp-featured, intrepid in social enterprise, and so truly British that she never knew when she was beaten, and never gave up when she was snubbed. And as they threaded their way through the throng of guests, he bowed and nodded upon all sides. For Mr. Poltimore-Briggs was possessed of the most admirable manners, — a different manner for each different man; so that toward the

great he behaved with deference, and to the
lesser folk with a dignity commensurate
with his great worth.

Close behind them came a young man in
tennis flannels and a blazer of blue.

So the Babblemouth people, as she had
called them, were come at last.   Impatient
to watch them upon their way toward her,
Miss Graham sat erect upon her throne, and
her bright eyes sparkled with delight.   But
the respectful bow and blandishment of
Poltimore-Briggs, who called her Helen,
and in his most affectionate manner inquired
after her health, passed unheeded.   The
voice of Mrs. Poltimore-Briggs, shrill in
respectful explanation, — "It was really so
unfortunate, but just as we were ready and
the carriage absolutely coming round to the
door, in came Sir John, and, of course,
having ridden ten miles, Henry could do no
less than — " although audible to the surrounding country, ran on unheard.   Miss
Graham's eyes and ears and thoughts were
all for this young man.

"Graham!" she said eagerly, holding

out both hands. "So you have come back."

"Yes, Aunt Helen. I came down yesterday."

For a full minute she looked at him attentively. "How well you are looking, boy!" she cried; and carried away by an impulse of affection, she placed a hand upon each shoulder, and, drawing him down toward her, warmly kissed him upon both cheeks.

The salute was not only unexpected but loud. The young man stood disconcerted, and blushed as if he had been smacked. He had an honest, open face, not over-clever, but fresh with sound health and ruddy from the open air. Then, as he smiled good-humouredly at the absurdity of the situation, a resemblance between himself and his aunt became very noticeable. He had the same frank look, the same grey eyes. His hair, which was clipped quite short, was fair, like the hair in the miniature.

"Sit down. Sit down and tell me about

yourself," she commanded in her quick way, pointing to the vacant chair by her side.

He obeyed at once. But his eyes wandered around the garden, narrowly scanning the groups of people, as if in search of some one whom he could not find.

Then she laid her hand upon his arm, and there was a little falter in her voice as she whispered, —

"But I must not keep you. You have not seen Charity yet. Come back and spend the evening when everybody is gone. There she is — in white — with the bishop — by the rhododendron."

He caught sight of her at last. A glance of understanding, a quick nod of dismissal from his aunt, and he rose and walked hastily across the lawn. She watched him tenderly as he spoke to the girl. And Charity turned and smiled, and looked quite glad. As they slowly strolled away together and disappeared amongst the trees, tears almost filled the little cripple's eyes. It was easy to guess the wish of her life.

But the cloud had risen above the cliff, and now the sunlight faded from the hill-side. A sudden gust of wind rushed up the coombe, and set the woods a-rustling with the rumour of a coming storm. Then something struck Miss Graham smartly upon the hand, and she looked down to find that her mitten was quite wet. And the bishop fancied he felt something, too, for he turned his classic shaven face toward heaven to ascertain whether it really rained. There was no room for doubt. A minute later the storm came down in torrents, and a sudden consternation seized the guests.

Poor Miss Graham!

Dowagers from the seats beside the yew hedge set stately sail; old boys came puffing like steam-tugs down the gravel paths, and men and maids went tacking in all directions, making for the house; but she sat still.

Mr. Poltimore-Briggs advanced with stately strides to Miss Graham's throne. "My dear Helen," he pleaded, in a tone of deep solicitude, "permit me to offer you an arm."

"No, no, thank you," she replied impatiently. "Let Sprake bring round my chair. Tell Sprake to bring round my chair."

She was keenly sensitive, and shrank from showing her infirmities. For the world she would not be seen to walk even those few yards. People would pity her, and the thought hurt her pride. But when at last she was solemnly wheeled to the French window, the drawing-room had already filled to overflowing; the hall was crowded, too, and guests stood under the portico disconsolately watching the pelting rain, which pattered down more and more. Mere men might laugh to see the heavens play this practical joke. But what can be done with more people than the house can hold? The women understood this, and, having shaken the raindrops from their skirts, whispered on all sides with deep feeling, —

"Poor Miss Graham! Poor Miss Graham!"

The lawn was empty now, suddenly

depopulated as a billiard-table after an eight stroke. Only two people remained out of doors. Like balls in the same pocket, they waited side by side under shelter of a tree. The white frock of Charity Chance and the flannels of Graham Poltimore stood clearly out from the sombre shadows of the copper beech. But the girl was ill at ease. She stepped hastily to the edge of the overhanging branches, and glanced up at the sky. A shower of rain-drops fell upon her, as leaning forward she struck the slanting leaves with the brim of her broad straw hat. The clouds looked hopeless and heavy as lead, and the storm poured down in torrents. Then she sighed as if she also echoed the sorrow, —

"Poor Miss Graham!"

The rector and the bishop had fore-gathered in the portico. The bishop had but recently returned from abroad, and may be pardoned the perplexity which knit his bushy eyebrows as he looked many years back into the past.

"I — eh — I remember old Dr. Graham.

He was a physician at Bath. A rather celebrated man in his day. But I can only recall — if my memory serve me aright — two daughters. One of them our good friend of to-day, and the other much younger, and a very beautiful girl — eh — as was universally admitted. She married Poltimore, much against her father's consent. A sort of — eh — runaway match, in fact, which attracted a great deal of attention at the time. Who, then, is this young lady — this niece whom they call Charity?"

The rector drew closer, as if not caring to be overheard.

"A child whom Miss Graham adopted and brought up. She lives with her as a sort of companion."

"And, eh, no relation?"

"Dear me, no — "

"She seemed to me a very charming young creature?" interrupted the bishop in a tone of inquiry, as if, on such a matter, his opinion might need corroboration.

"Yes. Yes, she is," replied the rector, briefly, as a matter of fact.

"And are they going to make a match of it?" laughed the bishop, pointing with elderly pleasantry toward the copper beech.

"I fear it is extremely likely. Capital young fellow, Poltimore. Might do a great deal better. Miss Graham has no one else with any claim upon her — no one whatever." Then the rector drew closer still, and his voice sank into a whisper. "It is rather a romantic story. The child was — "

"Charity Chance! Has any one seen Miss Chance? Miss Graham is asking for Miss Chance." It was Theodosia Mortimer who asked, and her voice sounded quite eager.

This inquiry, repeated by every tongue, cut short the rector's tale. The bishop glanced at the weather, stepped with alacrity into the hall, and took an umbrella from the stand. Thus equipped, he gaily embarked upon his mission. To the admiration of everybody, and the glory of his calves, he positively ran. He placed his paternal arm round her shoulder to hold the umbrella over her head, and thus

Charity was conveyed into the house with a tenderness and gallantry very beautiful in gaiters and a shovel hat.

But that was always the way. Strangers who talked to Charity and looked into her frank eyes felt a kindness for the girl.

In the hall she took off her hat, revealing the luxuriant wealth of her rich hair. She laughed to see the people sitting in pairs upon the stairs, as they sometimes do at a dance. But everybody was making merry of the mishap. People made room for her as she pushed her way to the other end of the drawing-room, where the little cripple was now installed. They turned to talk of her when she had passed. An atmosphere of wonder and curiosity surrounded this adopted daughter of the rich Miss Graham. The girl knew this, and it made her angry.

"Charity, dear" — the lace mittens were raised in a humorous gesture of despair — "we must do something for them — I want you to sing at once, child. But ballads, dear. Something quite simple, that they will all like."

"'Home, sweet Home,' I should think," laughed the girl, impatiently.

Upon the piano was a volume of "Songs of the West," a recent collection of the old ballads of that country, saved by a friendly hand at the last moment, ere they sank into oblivion. She had been singing them to please her own fancy. They were quaint, and fragrant of an old-world simplicity for which she was always looking and loved. Mrs. Poltimore-Briggs, who, by the bye, had once been a governess, volunteered to play the accompaniment.

The girl stood by the piano, facing the guests. She was restless and angry. It was a relief to stand up and do something — and she sang her best. She had been well taught, and her voice was low and sweet. Through the open door it filled the hall with the stairs, and even in the portico they could hear every syllable, —

"Down in the mead the other day,
 As carelessly I went my way,
 And plucked flowers red and blue,
 I little thought what love could do.

" I saw a rose with ruddy blush
And thrust my hand into the bush,
I pricked my fingers to the bone,
I would I 'd left that rose alone !

" I wish ! I wish ! but 't is in vain,
I wish I had my heart again !
With silver chain and diamond locks
I 'd fasten it in a golden box."

There is a tender melancholy about these old songs, both in the simple words and melody, which is irresistible, and goes straight to the heart. At the first note the conversation sank into a whisper and then died. As Charity finished, there was loud applause, and quite a chorus of voices: " If it is not asking too much, Miss Chance. If it is not troubling you, Charity — "

But the girl was as ready to sing as the birds in spring, from mere love of it. And so she went on, —

" The lily it shall be thy smock,
The jonquil shoe thy feet ;
Thy gown shall be the ten-week stock,
To make thee fair and sweet ; "

until at last the rain had passed over, and

again there came a sound of wheels upon
the gravel drive. Then Mrs. Poltimore-
Briggs was carried away by her lord; the
rector's lady went clucking around gather-
ing her daughters under her wing, and they
filed off as they had come; the bishop was
translated, and the rest went home. But
not one failed to congratulate Miss Graham,
and pour praises upon Charity Chance.
"Thank you so much" — "Such a *great*
treat" — "But I am not sure that the last
quite suits you, Charity," put in Theodosia.

"Capital! Very much obliged, Miss
Chance. Very much obliged, indeed,"
blurted the colonel of militia.

"Very charming," smiled the bishop.
But then the men admired Charity, and
meant it.

"Come here, child. Come here," beckoned Miss Graham, when they were all
gone. "Sit down on a corner of the foot-
stool. I am proud of you, dear. I am so
proud of you."

There was silence for a minute, whilst
the long, thin fingers kept stroking the
bright hair.

"And is not Graham looking well? Do
you know, I think he gets better looking
every time he comes down. Not so many
freckles — and the moustache improves him,
too. But he has such a nice face — an open
honest face — an English face."

The little lady brightened with enthusiasm as she pictured it. Then she bent
down and kissed the girl's white forehead.

"I asked him to come back by and by."

But Charity did not speak. She knew
the inner meaning of all this too well. And
although the words were not repeated, every
touch, every caress, and every smile was
only an echo of the familiar phrase, —

"But you know the wish of my life. You
know the one wish of my life."

CHAPTER III.

A PLIANT HOUR.

Upon the ceasing of the rain followed the sweetest eventide that ever lighted upon hill or sank beyond the sea. The pinks and mignonette were beaten down, the petals from the white rose lay strewn upon the ground. Yet the air never smelt so sweet, for the brown earth itself breathed forth a freshness and fragrance of its own. And every bird that had a tongue, from the thrush upon the tree-top to the blackbird hidden in the holly bush, burst into song.

So the party was over — thank goodness for that!

Miss Graham had gone upstairs, and Charity stole into the garden. She was quivering with emotion, and longed for the fresh air to cool her throbbing temples.

Up on a ladder by the window was John Sprake, putting a nail where the magnolia had been torn away by the storm.

"Massey 'pon us, Missie! There were a pity, to be sure," he shouted, at the top of his voice. "Why so much as ever you'd 'a' had time to zwank round like, and show one another your new vrocks, when comed down cats an' dogs. Made 'em turn tail an' run to hole like rabbits. Iss did. Ay, so did, sure 'nough."

A fine philosopher and observer of human manners, John Sprake. He was at Babblecombe before Charity, and she liked to talk to him. But now she hurried by without reply.

"Ay, put 'em out a bit. I'll warr'nt did. So 't would, sure 'nough," he chuckled to himself, as he turned to the wall.

She strode quickly into the shrubbery, where the high bushes hid her on all sides. Alone at last, her pent-up indignation found a voice. What did these people mean who looked upon her so coldly? They were no better than she. Better, indeed! There was no one of them could do anything she could not do. And yet, in some indefinable way, they slighted her as a person of small account. Because she was an orphan — adopted, brought up on charity. Her spirit rose in revolt against the narrowness of this little Babblemouth world. She hated them all — every one. Her heart told her there was a nobility of which they knew nothing — somewhere, beyond this little coombe — in the great city, perhaps. She was not one with these people. She was not of the same blood. She longed to meet a human soul suffering disadvantage, to give sympathy and receive it. As to Theodosia Mortimer, *she* wanted Graham Poltimore, and made eyes at him. That was at the bottom of her behaviour.

She walked restlessly on. At the end of the path a wicket gate opened into the wood, and against this she leaned. The place was quite solitary, and she remained so still that a rabbit in the copse went on feeding undisturbed, a few yards from her feet.

Graham Poltimore loved her madly —

she had no doubt of it. He gave her no peace, and she could no longer procrastinate. On the April morning with the sun shining between the clouds, when he came to say "Good-by," his last whisper had been of love. To-day, on his return, his first words beneath the copper beech were a passionate appeal.

It was heartless to refuse a love like that. She thought she could almost love him if he would only leave her alone, or do something more than hunt or shoot, and hope that he might just scrape through — as he called it — something noble and great — that she could worship. She would have him a scholar — a soldier. In fact she did not want to marry — unless —

To hear the Mortimer girls, one would think there was no aim in life but to catch a husband by hook or by crook, and she hated that. Her dream was of an irresistible passion, carrying all before it. Then an icy fear swept over her like a northeast wind. She had no feeling, no heart, no soul, no gratitude. That was why people were cold to her. That was why she did not return Graham's love.

Yet surely she did love Graham Poltimore. How could it be otherwise? When last winter a returning huntsman, riding slowly through the coombe, left word that young Poltimore had been thrown and hurt, did her heart hesitate? She blushed to think how she had run breathless into Babble-mouth — so that even now people tattled and laughed. They said she wanted to catch Graham Poltimore — the fools! Sour-faced Mrs. Mortimer warned her of this — out of kindness, as she said.

The voice of John Sprake broke in upon her thoughts. Her ear could not distinguish the words, but his sing-song shouting seemed to fill the coombe. Miss Graham might be asking for her. She must go in.

At thought of the little cripple, tears came into the girl's eyes.

The golden eventide rested like a crown upon the head of the wood; and every sentiment which could soften her into acquiescence burst into life and warmth within her bosom.

Dear Miss Graham! How good she had always been! And this marriage would be the one perfect joy of her life, — the happy ending to an idyl which was no mere dream of the imagination, but a story in living flesh and blood. For Miss Graham had created her — made her what she was — brought her up as a flower with infinite tenderness, sheltered from the wind of adversity and protected from the biting frost of the world's unkindness. For such a friend could any sacrifice be too great? And she was capable of sacrifice — adored it, longed for it — some great and noble sacrifice! If *he* had been the cripple she would have married him without a moment's doubt, only to comfort his crumpled form against her bosom.

Suddenly the rabbit in the pathway raised itself alert and listened.

If she married him, her future was secure. He, at least, did not care who she was and whence she came. He was too generous for that. How angry all the Mortimers would be — at first, and then obsequious.

3

There came a quick step upon the gravel. She turned, and he was by her side.

He had walked quickly, and his face glowed with health and careless irresponsibility.

"Sprake told me you were in the garden, Charity," he burst out, "and I came to find you at once. I was afraid you might be indoors, and that I should not see you alone at all."

"I was just going in," she interrupted him nervously, turning toward the house.

"But not now. Not until you have told me. Charity, I think of nothing else. It is the dream of my life. I cannot live without you. And I cannot go on like this without knowing. If it is hopeless, you must say so. I come and go — at Easter I came down and went again; but you manage — you always manage — to evade me. I cannot go on like this. If you know you will never love me, I will go away and never come back. I will turn my back upon the place forever and go abroad. I do not care what happens to me — whether I live or die —"

In his excitement, words failed him. He had spoken with the wild exaggeration of young romance, and yet it was all so real. How madly he worshipped her! A womanly pity pleaded for him against her doubt. It were no better than heartless cruelty to remain unmoved by such a love as that.

"But I am not sure," she faltered, "that I — that I care for you enough for that."

"But you love me a little."

"I am very fond of you, Graham," she replied, in a firmer voice. "You have always known that. But it seems different. Not like what you mean. Not like what you say you feel yourself."

"But that will come — that will come," he urged eagerly.

"If I could be sure of that!"

The cry leapt straight from her heart, and was tender with regret. There were so many reasons why she should love, that this coldness troubled her.

"Charity!" he cried passionately, "how can you doubt it? You do love me, I know you do. I can hear it in your voice; and you say yourself you are fond of me. We were made for each other, and it is the one wish of poor Aunt Helen's heart. Why should we delay? It is not as if we could marry to-morrow, and I were asking you to bind yourself beyond all recall. But promise me now. Let us go in and tell her to-night. She will be glad beyond everything. And I will make you happy, Charity. I love you so much I cannot help making you happy."

His words almost persuaded her; but she remained silent, and turned to lean against the gate again.

"Let me tell her, Charity — "

"No, no," she answered, in a voice low but very clear. "Do not say a word, Graham. But if you want to please me very much, go away quite early, and I will tell her myself."

He could scarcely believe in his good fortune.

"Then — then, we are engaged?" he cried.

"Yes.   I suppose we are engaged."

He threw his arm around her neck and would have kissed her. But she drew back.

"Not now — not now, Graham dear," she said quickly. "Come, let us go into the house. There is the bell."

CHAPTER IV.

THE MINIATURE.

THEY were in the drawing-room, and a maid was bringing in the lamp, when Graham Poltimore rose to go. He had scarcely spoken to his father since his return, he said; and Miss Graham accepted the explanation without one word of question. During dinner conversation had been scanty, and the little lady's quick grey eyes, glancing from one to another, became at first perplexed and then sad. She felt that something had happened, and to her, as well as Charity, his departure came as a relief.

"You may leave the shutters awhile," she said, turning to the maid with nervous impatience. "The room becomes so warm when the windows are closed. Bring the book, Charity, and come and sit by me."

It was customary every night for the girl to read or sing, and sometimes they remained quite late, forgetful of time and place in the bright illusions of poetry and romance. Beside the sofa where they sat, upon a small round table, stood the lamp. But to-night the reading was slow to begin. Charity waited long, the book unopened in her hand.

"Did you mark the place, dear?" asked Miss Graham, with quiet self-repression; then, melting into sudden tenderness, she drew the girl toward her and fell to stroking the bright hair.

"Never mind, child," she whispered sadly. "I understand it all quite well. When I longed for it so much, I only meant if it could really be — not against your heart's inclination, dear — not if it harboured a doubt. Nothing can ever lessen my affection for you, Charity, — nothing. You may always rest assured of that."

"But you do not understand, aunt. Graham asked me again to-night, and I accepted him."

"Then why did he go?"

"I wanted to tell you myself — all alone."

"And you are quite happy?"

"More than happy."

It was true. The delicacy of those tender assurances had gone straight to Charity's heart. They touched her deeply, and in an ecstasy of gratitude and gladness she threw her arms around the little cripple's neck. What if this promise were a sacrifice? The very doubt, which just now held her halting, filled her soul with joy. She also had something to give, — some return to make for these years of kindness. She was conferring happiness upon the human being she most loved. Her quick, tell-tale face, ever ready to betray emotion, glowed with triumph at the thought.

To little Miss Graham this was all natural. She interpreted that look of joy in her own manner. Her eyes beamed brighter than ever, as they filled with tears of joy.

"Charity, darling!" she cried, with wild excitement and delight, "it has made every-thing right. All I have will be Graham's some day. Half of it should be his now, in justice to his mother. And he shall have it at once. There is no need to wait. Let him go back and get his degree, and you can be married next summer. I know what love is. There shall be no long engagement. I know what love is — at second-hand — always at second-hand."

As she repeated the words, her voice sank into a wail of regret; then she paused a moment, and went on in a deep, rapid whisper, —

"Charity, I cannot help talking to you to-night. Within this wretched, misshapen little body is a real woman's heart. It makes no difference, child. It is some-thing of the soul. For the most perfect that ever walked under God's sun had no more capacity for loving, no greater longing to be loved, than I, who only hobble from chair to sofa or hide my back and truckle along the road on wheels. I tell you, child, I was made living, and knew that I could never live."

Again she stopped. Her thin fingers eagerly unpinned the miniature upon her breast, and she held it toward the lamp, gazing lovingly upon the face.

"Look, Charity! Look at her, child! She loved. How she used to come and tell me! You could never have taken her for my sister, — so well-grown and graceful. But she hurt me; without knowing it, she hurt me. She would talk of him by the hour, and always as if I could not understand. Yet it was I who did it when they thwarted her. She could only sit and cry. She had given way until I stirred her into revolt, and quickened her with my spirit. And so she followed her heart's desire, and married Poltimore in spite of all. What is it Thekla sings, child?

"'*Ich habe genossen das irdische Glück,
Ich habe gelebt und geliebet!*'

But what a little while she lived! And I, the
useless one, to stay on all these years!"

With a sigh she laid down the portrait
upon the table, and, turning toward the
girl, placed a hand upon each shoulder.

"After she had gone, the loneliness fell
heavy upon me. It haunted the quiet,
proud old house; the street was full of it,
where everybody was astir, so quick and
strong. Her marriage was a madness, they
said. I was not even allowed to speak her
name. One night a letter came; that was
when Graham was born, and as I sat thinking there crept into my heart a longing.
I knew that I, too, was made for mater-
nity, — I, who was never to bear a child.
I wanted to know. I wanted to feel
the warmth of it upon my bosom. And
every day it grew and grew from a little
loneliness to a great despair: until at
last I found you, child. And ever since
my one thought has been set upon to-
day. Year by year I watched you grow
up like a flower — and waited. You were
so bright and warm, I could put my cheek

against your hair and feel the day coming when you would love and live and learn it all. The hope kept my heart young. The touch of you kept my blood warm. It was like food and fire to keep a starving soul alive. And now you are to marry, — you two, who are all the world to me. Kiss me, Charity. It shall be next year, and you shall live here. Kiss me, dear. I planned it all from the day when you first ran. And he has grown up such a man! Only sometimes I feared he did not care enough about things — books and poetry, I mean — to please you. Do you feel it cold, child?"

She stopped abruptly, and glanced toward the still open window. A great moth had come in and was fluttering around the lamp. Moonlight fell across the lawn and glistened upon the dark beech-tree. The rain had left a humid chilliness in the night air. But not from that did the girl shiver. The eagerness of the little cripple's words had moved her sympathies and made her shake like an aspen.

"No, no," she said quickly; "the air is close."

"Yet shut it up; and at the same time ring. We will not read to-night. It has been a long and wearying day — but a glad day, Charity, both for you and me."

"Yes, the gladdest of all," cried the girl, carried away by her emotion.

"My stick has fallen. Come, give me your arm, dear, and we will go upstairs. You must be tired too."

But Charity was not tired. Alone in her room she sat down in the square window, quaintly projecting over the porch, and curtained off like another chamber. Never was sleep further from her eyelids. Never were her senses more alert. The slanting moonlight glanced between blind and mullion, and she eagerly drew each cord, until a flood of light filled the place from floor to ceiling. She looked down the quiet coombe at the roof of sleeping Babble-mouth. Upon one higher than the rest, standing just under the hill, the smooth slates were shining like silver. How well she knew it — that largest house in the little town — the home of the "Babblemouth people;" to-night it stood out from the rest with an import strange and new.

Half-way over the gap and above the open sea hung the full moon.

Neither fleeing cloud nor passing ship broke the serenity or burst in upon the solitude. The ragged bushes on the brow of the cliff lay flat and dark against the sky, and nothing moved but the broken ripple of the running tide, where the moonbeams danced down a broad trackway, into the harbour mouth. The hollow under the hill lay hidden in gloom and mystery.

Many times before she had looked out upon this moonlit sea, but to-night transcended all experience. The surpassing beauty held her senses captive, — the wonder stirred her soul to some unknown, unfathomed depth.

Graham Poltimore's words came whirling through her memory, "Charity, I think of nothing else. I cannot live without you."

The reality of his passion startled her. It agitated her like a wild strain of some strange music once heard and wanting interpretation. But it awakened no responsive echo in her heart.

There was no triumph in this love. For him she felt a pity of the imagination, and for herself a fear. And the passionate yearning of her helpless little friend, longing for more than life could give, haunted her like a sad, sad song.

Her intention did not waver. She loved these people both, and would make them happy. One way lay before her, straight and clear as that path of light, and she knew of no other. But there had come to her an undefined longing for something beyond all she knew. She stood there, still in her white frock, until the moon had sunk behind the sea and the great black cliffs grew dim.

CHAPTER V.

MERE MONEY MATTERS.

A STRANGE mixture of fine feeling and fastidious sensibility was this little lady of Babblecombe House. She dwelt in a garden of poetry — a sort of fairy island of her own — where, alas! at times she suffered rude shocks from the tempests that sweep across the sea of life. Then she cowered in a corner until her sorrow was forgotten in sunshine and flowers, as the garden bloomed afresh.

It was a heavy blow when her father died unreconciled to Irene. Good repute and the respectful admiration of Bath constituted the breath of that great physician's professional nostrils, and the scandal of his girl's elopement went near to break his

heart. He scented the pump-room gossip.
He detected the covert smiles of rival
medical practitioners, and they made him
mad. In reality he felt these more deeply
than the loss of his daughter, although
Irene had been a belle in Bath, as the good
bishop remembered. In his wrath he swore
that rascal Poltimore should never touch a
penny of his money.

But in little more than a year, stepping
from his brougham to pay a visit, he
dropped suddenly upon the wide pavement
in Milson Street, and neither spoke nor
opened his eyes upon the world again.

In her loneliness Helen Graham sent
post-haste for her sister, who hurried home
to the great shuttered house, bringing
Graham, a baby in arms. How good to be
restored to each other! They wept together
— in sorrow for the dead, in joy of the
new-born.

But Dr. Graham had kept his word.
After the funeral it was found that every
farthing was left in trust for "my daughter
Helen," with power of appointment to her

by will. She could not part with the money during life, although she could leave it as she would.

Between baser spirits this must have opened an impassable gulf, but it seemed only to knit the sisters in closer affection. They spoke of it with bated breath, scarcely daring to call in question the justice of the dead or defeat his intention. After all, the money might have been lost, which now must be secured to little Graham. Bless him! And meanwhile Helen could pay Irene's bills. Then, to be near her sister, the little cripple bought the mansion at Babblecombe, with the cottages, the wood, and the small farm let with the mill. Scarcely had she come there to live, when Irene died.

For a while sorrow brought closer intimacy between the bereaved neighbours. Helen Graham was constantly driving into the town to the little motherless boy. And Henry Poltimore, then agent to Lord Babblemouth, and steward to his lordship's vast estates, was no less frequently at

Coombe. She could not do without him.
He advised her concerning the mill, the
cottage, and the farm. She esteemed him
highly. She pitied him with all her heart.
And if at times a manner somewhat too
large jarred upon her nerves, — as when he
boasted of his own gentility, or talked of
his lordship at unnecessary length, — such
little matters must be forgiven to a man of
business. She had always understood dis-
creet reserve and perfect self-restraint to be
the exclusive possessions of upper professional circles, and the pick of the aris-
tocracy. As a man of affairs, as a man of
heart, Henry Poltimore was perfect; and
he also had loved and lost Irene.

About this time one of the trustees under
her father's will was called to his last
account. She gladly appointed Henry
Poltimore. Who so fit to accept this trust
as the father of the child to whom the
property should some day fall? This was
reasonable, and readily agreed to by the
remaining trustee.

Then suddenly came a blow which shook

her soul's belief in human nature to its profoundest depths.

It was delivered by Mrs. Mortimer, then the rector's young bride, who one morning hurried panting from Babblemouth, and entered the French window as pale as Hamlet's ghost. Not that she was affected by the news she bore; but driven by excitement, and a laudable desire to be friendly and tell Miss Graham first, she had travelled with inexpedient speed.

"Mr. Henry Poltimore has married again!" she gasped.

"Married again! When? Where? To whom?"

"To a governess — in Wiltshire — they say she is the daughter of a farmer — "

"The daughter of a farmer," interrupted Miss Graham, indignantly; "I do not believe it! He is broken-hearted! He is inconsolable!"

"But he has written to the rector. He could not bear the solitude, he said. They married quietly — nine in the morning — none present, because Mr. Poltimore is still in mourning. The rector thinks it positively indecent. So very soon, you know. You will certainly get a letter when the post comes. But I thought you would like to know at once."

It was too true. The prediction was little sooner uttered than confirmed, for the postman was already upon the gravel path.

"He might at least have married a lady," said Miss Graham, with bitter self-control. But her hand shook, and the letter dropped upon the floor.

That was all she said. It was reported in Babblemouth, and afterwards repeated to the second Mrs. Poltimore, on the authority of the rector's wife. But although she sat in her chair, stiff with dignity, tears rushed into her eyes at the thought of Irene, sweet and beautiful as an angel, and only a few months in heaven.

She was too proud to give expression to her pain. When Mr. Poltimore brought home his bride, she called. But her constant visits were discontinued. They must send over the little boy on every fine, warm

day, she told them. She should be pleased
to welcome them at Babblecombe at any
time, of course, but she had given up going
out. Thus they sank into comparative
insignificance as "the Babblemouth people."
A little later, in spite of their remonstrance, she adopted Charity Chance; an
act of benevolence which so far had
brought her nothing but happiness and
love.

Then Mr. Henry Poltimore suddenly
became rich, retired from his stewardship,
and blossomed into Briggs. He bought a
small estate close to Babblemouth, and
farmed it to the admiration of surrounding
agriculturists. It was like a garden. "But,
la! it never couldn't pay," they said. He
bred prize cattle of marvellous length of
pedigree and price, and rented the shooting
of Babblemouth Park when his Lordship
went abroad, and added a wing to his house,
and built new stables, which everybody
said were better than most people's cottages.
The hillside above the town glistened
with his conservatories; and his grapes,

exhibited at all the flower shows, became the despair of every gardener in the west.

Thus he grew and grew, and many people thought he ought to be made a magistrate for the county. He thought so himself. His devotion to public business deserved no less. For he sat on every board and council in the district, and spoke, too, at considerable length. Thus his name was in every mouth. As elections were frequent, it brightened every hoarding, and enlivened every blank wall in the neighbourhood. Gate-posts bloomed perennially with invitations to "Vote for Poltimore-Briggs." And what a friend he was — a friend to the farmer — a friend to the landed interest — a friend to the poor man. Nothing was too high or too low to be included in the friendship of Poltimore-Briggs. And at last this broad humanity, assisted by persistent pushing of himself, was to reap its reward. The Agricultural Association had determined to run a candidate for Parliament, and upon whom should its maiden fancy light but Mr. Poltimore-Briggs!

No wonder, when at last he was left sole surviving trustee, Miss Graham did not appoint another. Such a thought could not enter her head. For everything was managed to perfection. Her dividends were never a day late; not even the rent of a cottage went into arrears.

Some days had elapsed, and the buzz of excitement following Charity's engagement had settled down. It was a lovely summer morning, and John Sprake had already toiled half-way up the hill, when Miss Graham suddenly leaned forward in her chair.

"Have the horses been exercised, John?"

John Sprake, who, although a very steady man, was no fool, hearing himself thus addressed, speedily turned around the little wheel, and respectfully rested.

In Miss Graham's opinion, nobody in this world was so good as John Sprake — in his own station in life, of course. Nobody could pull the chair like John Sprake. She could trust no other in the same way, for several excellent reasons. He was a coachman, and understood driving, and had never been known to go fast or have an accident in his life. He was clean-shaved, with white, wavy hair, which reminded her of the late Dean of Bath. He had buried two wives, poor man, and married a third; and brought up fourteen children and lost four; and looked very respectable in church in top-boots and a blue livery; and, during his whole twenty years of service, had never done anything giddy or lost his head. Therefore she placed implicit confidence in John Sprake.

"Regularly?" She looked him keenly in the face. Something evidently weighed upon her mind.

Ever so small a spot upon John's conscience made him unduly to protest.

"Iss, mum. Every day so sure as the sun — zo to speak — unless 't is vor some good reason."

"And are they in good order?"

"Zo vat 's butter."

"Yes, but I mean quite quiet?"

"Zo quiet 's mice."

"Then bring round the carriage this afternoon at three.   Miss Chance is going for a
sail, and I shall drive into town with her."

This unexpected termination to a cross-
examination, pressing perilously close upon
detection, took John Sprake's breath away.
As he explained at leisure, when subsequent proceedings attracted attention in
the village: "I wur that tookt aback, that
wh'er or no I wur 'pon my head or my
heels I could n' ha' told.   There!   If you'd
'a' stuck Jan Sprake wi' a knife, thik
minute, he would n' never ha' blood."

However, he managed to murmur, "Iss,
mum," and turned and plodded wisely on
his way.

No wonder the man was startled.   Jan
Sprake bestriding one fat carriage-horse and
leading another was the most familiar
object in the Babblecombe landscape.   He
did very little else, and many a distasteful
duty did John avoid by urging the imme-
diate necessity to exercise his horses.   He
had been known to refuse to haul the chair
because he must take out his horses.   And

this with such a serious shake of his hoary old head that the poor little woman was nearly moved to tears by the contemplation of such devotion to dumb animals. She had not set foot in a carriage for years. The splendid chariot, its wheels picked out with yellow, and the brougham in which her distinguished father formerly paid his visits, stood in the coach-house side by side, in solemn state. She would not have parted with them for the world. Sometimes a visitor must be fetched from the station, five miles over the hill, and the mere thought of a hired fly made her shudder. But ten years ago, when alighting, she had stumbled and fallen in Babblemouth street; and since then, except upon those rare occasions, the carriages had remained at rest.

But with Charity's engagement, over everything had come a change.

The little lady started life anew. Her tenderest hope, hitherto liable to be cut off by any frost, was at last hardened into a set purpose. She could look forward to flowers and fruit.

Of late a doubt had often troubled her mind. If Charity did not marry Graham, she must be provided for in some manner consistent with the luxury in which she had been brought up. To educate and then to leave her poor would be cruelty indeed, — for education, in the opinion of this little lady, added a grace only. It was not meant for the work-a-day world. Common people were better without it, with its restless, upsetting influences, leading only to discontent. And the pay which an accomplished lady could command was a mere pittance. Yet to leave money away from her own kin seemed to savour of robbery, and was scarcely a righteous act. She almost fancied it might follow her beyond the grave, and meet with disapproval both in this world and the next. For in this woman's heart was a fair mixture of fine old family pride.

But now that Charity was to be her niece indeed, all doubts were blown to the winds. People called, letters came by every post, and the very air became quite bracing with congratulation. In her joy, with every hour Miss Graham evolved a new and loftier idea. Graham should add the name of Graham, as his father had taken Briggs, and Charity become the mother of a fresh line of Grahams. It was a noble mission. Only to think of it brought the colour to the little cripple's cheek. The girl whom she had always loved so well was now worshipped, and this order for the carriage was an act of sacrifice and devotion.

To the intensity of this new-found fervour witnessed every word and look. The reality of it unconsciously impressed John Sprake so that he hauled and wheeled in silence, without stopping for argument or rest.

Nor did his wisdom afterward invent any specious obstacle; and the carriage was brought round upon the stroke of three.

"Put the footstool closer, Charity dear, and draw the shawl over my shoulder! To Mr. Poltimore-Briggs's, Sprake."

Thus she courageously started; but all along the Babblemouth road, and down the one street which forms the town, she nervously clutched the girl's hand. Tradesmen, scarcely able to believe their eyes, popped to their shop doors to be sure it was Miss Graham who passed. Two of the rector's daughters upon the causeway turned back at once, to carry home the news. Quite a little crowd of children gathered round as the carriage drew up before the house of Poltimore-Briggs.

A large house of red brick, three stories high, with a paved court in front, enclosed with tall iron railings against the raised causeway. An old-fashioned, ornamental arch of wrought iron, bearing an heraldic shield and a square frame to hold a lamp, bent over the gates. The windows were long and narrow, with thick sash-bars; and above the brass knocker on the front door, in places of panels, were panes of glass to light the hall. It was a fine old place, this ancient house of some forgotten merchant; and above the brass knocker it frowned down upon street and harbour with the solemn dignity of a bygone age.

Scarcely had the carriage stopped, when the door quickly opened and Poltimore-Briggs himself came hurrying hatless down the steps and across the paved court. He was carefully attired, as at the garden party; his face shone with pleasure, and his bald head glistened in the sun.

"Now this is kind; Helen, this is delightful. Let me help you. Take care of the step—" Suddenly remembering Charity, he gave her his hand without looking at her, still talking all the while. "I saw you from the window, and could hardly believe my eyes. But you are in no hurry. You will stay. Sprake must put up the horses. Yes. Put up the horses, Sprake. Really not? Then wait, Sprake. Take care, Helen, take care. The polished floor is slippery—"

And so, with blusterous zeal, he led her across the hall, bending down that she might take his arm.

"You have come at a fortunate moment," he cried, unable to conceal his pride. "I have been invited to stand for Parliament.

A deputation — a most influential deputation, from one of the most powerful organisations in the division — has just left me. You must have passed them in the street. I admit I was gratified — deeply gratified. But I have not yet given a reply. We shall find the others in the new room — "

"I wanted to talk to you," she whispered, in that sudden way of hers which sounded so abrupt.

"To be sure. To be sure. Let us go in here. We shall be alone. You'll find the others, Charity, somewhere or other. They are waiting for you, and the boat is ready. Graham has an old school friend with him. A poet or something of the sort, so they say. Alfred — Alfred Prentice."

As a man of affairs, he laughed at the bare idea of poetry. Then, as he opened the door, he added with respect: "But I've seen his name in the papers."

They went into a large dining-room with three tall windows looking out upon the street. It was panelled half-way up the walls, and furnished with pieces of old oak, picked up during many years at sales in the neighbourhood. It had an odd look, as if it belonged not to the place, — this flotsam from the seas of bankruptcy and death. Many of the chairs were out of place, and on the long oak table stood empty decanters and glasses, to prove how well the thirsty deputation had refreshed itself. Over the mantel-piece hung a life-sized portrait of Poltimore-Briggs himself, smiling round at a visitor, pen in hand, and upon his face a light of intelligence such as, without the advantage of baldness, human forehead dare not hope to sustain. The attitude was justified; the quill no mere poetic flight. In the local newspaper he had once waged bitter war, the Incidence of Local Taxation being the theme.

The paint upon the picture was scarcely dry, but a host of old familiar objects recalled the past. A bookcase from the old house in Bath; a pencil drawing, by an artist of that city, of Irene, a school-girl, with hair half-way down her back, — these moved the little woman deeply, and for a

while after she was seated she did not
speak.

But Poltimore-Briggs blustered heed-
lessly on: —

"Why, it must be twenty years, Helen,
since you were last here. Did you notice
we 've thrown the little room into the hall?
A wonderful improvement, I flatter myself.
Some of the deputation said frankly they
had never seen anything carried out so
thoroughly and well. You must look when
you go out. And you would n't know the
gardens now. I don't know what I 've
spent upon them, I 'm sure. Thousands!
More than I was justified. More than I
shall ever see again. Lord Babblemouth
came in only the other day — when he was
down about the new quay. He wanted my
advice — he thinks a deal of my opinion —
and he was astonished. He said, ' Poltimore ' — he said — he always forgets and
calls me Poltimore still — ' Poltimore, you
have the prettiest place in the west of Eng-
land — for the size, of course.' I said, ' I
am gratified to find you like it, my Lord.'

And so I was, I confess. And so it ought to be, for it costs a pretty penny to keep it up. Four men summer and winter, and sometimes five in the spring."

He paused for some note of admiration, some expression of surprise, and looked larger than ever, with his hands thrust in the pockets of his white waistcoat. But little Miss Graham had scarcely heard his words. Only when he ceased she became conscious of what he had been saying.

"I have something to tell you, Henry," she began, and her voice was tremulous and very low. "A secret that you must not repeat. I only tell you now because I want something done. I should have sent for you to come over if I had not seen you to-day. I have been thinking over it for some time, and I want your help and advice."

Her earnestness arrested his attention; she was shaking from an agitation she tried in vain to repress.

"You know, Helen," he replied in his

large way, with a wave of the hand, "that I am always at your service. I —"

"Yes. Yes. You have been very kind. You have been most good; but — but —" She paused, in doubt how to begin, and then, summoning all her courage, continued: "Do you remember the story of the Spartan boy who concealed a fox in his bosom?"

He nodded assent. She has found out that rascal Sprake, he said to himself. For in his mind was the fable of the man who cherished a snake, and he thought it meant ingratitude.

"And then it gnawed into his heart, and he died."

"What do you mean, Helen? What do you mean?"

"I want to arrange and settle everything without delay. I have known it for some time. But I could not speak of it. And I do not want any one to know. Henry, I have only a little while to live. Perhaps two years at most. Only two years to live."

Her voice sank into a wail. But now that her sorrow had found utterance she at once regained composure, and she looked up with her keen grey eyes, as if eager to observe the effect upon him of her words.

He was standing upon the hearth-rug, and the light from one of the windows fell full upon his face. His brows were knit in perplexity, as if he did not quite catch her meaning, but the colour left his cheek. He became pale with alarm. He could not have appeared more startled had he just heard his own doom.

"Do you mean you are ill, Helen?" he asked eagerly, in a hoarse whisper.

"Beyond hope. There is no chance of recovery," she moaned. Then she burst into passionate lament: "And I do not want to die. I want to live. I want to live for years and years."

"But what are you doing? Why don't you take advice? Call in Bibberly. He's a good man, Bibberly. I should have every confidence, and —"

"Do you think I would have such as he

prying at my poor body?" she cried, with sudden nervous irritability. "No. I wrote to a physician at Bath. I sent Charity out for the day, and John Sprake fetched and drove him back, and nobody knew. Besides, I have read about it in one of my father's books. Nothing can be done. He did not propose anything. It must just grow and grow. I can see it grow."

"But — eh, surely — " he hesitated, groping in his brain for the thing to say. "Surely, Helen, you will take a second opinion?"

"It is no good. Besides, they might want to do something."

She shuddered at the thought, and then again came upon her this great longing for life.

"And yet I do not want to go. I could not lose it for the world, little as it is. To be wheeled out into the sun. To watch in winter for the Christmas roses in the corner. And the daffodils in spring, so bright in the meadow along the brook. And the bluebells in the wood, quite thick, as if the sky had fallen between the trees. And I want to see Charity married — and to sit like a grandmother, with children running around my chair. There are people who say they are tired of life — people who have it all. But I was never tired. I could never do enough to get tired."

She stopped in her sudden way, and asked quickly: "You were not averse to Graham's engagement?"

The look of fear vanished from his countenance. The question implied a doubt, and again he was important and self-satisfied as ever.

"I will not seek to hide from you, Helen," he began slowly, and in his most sententious manner, as if he were addressing a Board of Guardians, "that I had cherished other hopes for Graham. My position and his — his expectations, I think I may say, justified me in hoping that he would make a suitable match. I was ambitious for him, I confess to you. It was only natural. Personally, I say nothing against Miss Chance. Thanks to your bounty, she is well brought up, intelligent, accomplished — but — "

"You would be too generous to speak of that," she broke in with warmth.

He graciously accepted the attribute: "Well, well! Graham has chosen, and we need say no more."

With his patronising wave of the hand he would have dismissed the matter, but she had still her errand to fulfil.

"But I want to see everything clear. I love her as if she were my own, and I want to know that whatever happens she will be provided for," she cried with glowing enthusiasm. "Of course I have left all to Graham, and that is only just. But there is the money that has been saved. That seems to me quite different. I want to give her that at once. To settle, or secure, or whatever you call it. So that it can never be lost or taken away, you know. Now, in my lifetime, I want to do it. So that if anything comes between them she will have it just the same. And when they marry, it can make no difference."

He turned to the window, and stood with his back toward her, looking out into the street. She felt that he disapproved of her intention. The old opposition, she thought, offered to poor Charity from the very first. This made her more determined.

"You see," she urged, "I do not want to have to think of these things again. Soon I may have to tell Charity, and I want all this settled first. As if it were for the marriage, and as much for his sake as hers."

He walked slowly back, and leaned with his elbow upon the mantel-piece. He looked ten years older than the portrait now, and the lines upon his forehead were very deep.

"I have been taken by surprise, and what you tell me of yourself pains me very deeply, Helen," he faltered. "Let the matter rest. I will think how your wishes can be best carried out. Leave it for the present. Leave it; I will not forget nor delay. But such things want looking at — careful looking at — "

There came a step across the hall — the door was thrown open, and Mrs. Poltimore-Briggs, like a little whirlwind out of breath, broke in upon their conference. She was full of regrets, and overflowing with apologies. Her rapid trivialities, pitched in the highest key of exaggeration, were in strange contrast to the deep sorrow hidden in Miss Graham's heart.

"My dear Miss Graham! How could he bring you into this disreputable room? I was beside myself when Charity mentioned it. I rushed away at once in the most frantic haste. Why, you must be quite worn out and exhausted. Now do let me take you into the other room to have some tea! Let me take your arm. I won't trust you to him any longer. Open the other window, Henry, do. It is as close as an oven."

So the interview came abruptly to a close, and he was left alone.

The cool air blowing in from the sea was grateful to him, and he stood looking down upon the harbour mouth. It was high-tide;

but below the clear, deep water he could distinguish lighter streaks of sand between masses of weed-covered rocks. There came a moment of insight. Between the whirling eddies of his vanity, and the varying agitations of his social ambition, he caught glimpses of the unchanging realities of life.

In his perplexity he passed his hand across his forehead. It was wet with beads of perspiration.

"Two years! Two years!" he muttered. "He must marry her at once."

Between the cliffs lay a cutter in readiness to go out. He could hear the creaking of her gaff and the hoops of her mainsail against the mast, as it flapped idly when she rolled upon the swell of the tide.

Two members of the deputation strolled down, and stood upon the quay. One of them, in gaiters and with a back of the broadest acreage, raised his stick and pointed at her.

He knew that they were talking of him — saying, perhaps with envy, that she was his. An hour before he would have been gratified, — very gratified; but now the thought was bitter to him.

"I wish to God I was dead and in my grave!" he hissed between his teeth. And at that moment he meant it too.

CHAPTER VI.

ALFRED PRENTICE.

A POET? Alfred Prentice? Yes, there sometimes appeared verses in the magazines signed with that name. Charity had seen, but scarcely read them, or if so they left no deep impression on her mind. But the mere thought of a poet made her heart quicken with interest and enthusiasm. In her restless impatience with Babblemouth and its trivialities, one thing she longed for more than all, — intercourse with people whose minds were lifted above littlenesses upon great ideas. No poet had ever been known in Babblemouth, except the little shoemaker on the quay, who recommended inelegant boots in limping verse, and drove a thriving trade in consequence.

Attracted by the sound of voices, she went quickly down a long passage to a door at the back of the house. It opened into a paved court at the foot of a terrace, beyond which a large walled garden ran up the hillside.

Here in the cool several people were seated. Theodosia Mortimer, with her mother and some of her sisters, Mrs. Poltimore-Briggs and Graham. They had gathered in a semicircle around a stranger, who leaned back in his chair smoking a cigarette. Upon the ground close to his hand, which hung over the arm of the chair, lay a small red volume he had just put down.

As she came into the doorway, Charity was greeted with a chorus of mingled welcome and regret.

"We are ready and waiting for you, Charity," said Mrs. Mortimer, with her never-ceasing smile.

"Oh, Charity! What a pity you were not here before! You have lost the most delightful treat," piped Mrs. Poltimore-Briggs. "Mr. Prentice has been good enough to read us one of his most beautiful poems."

"And you so fond of poetry too," chimed in Theodosia.

The poet languidly rose from his seat, and stood in an attitude combining ease with angularity.   Less than the middle height, and very slight, beside Graham Poltimore he looked quite small.   His hair, of which there was a great deal, was black as jet; his shaven face thin and pale, and his eyes large and bright.   He wore a soft hat, a velvet jacket, and a lace cravat.

At the first glance there came to Charity a strange feeling of mistrust, — an intuition of something new and not yet understood, which brought the colour to her cheek, and caused her to abruptly turn away.   "How happy she looks, now she is engaged!" thought Theodosia Mortimer.   "What luck the girl has had!"

In the movement and flutter of excitement, for a moment the poet seemed likely to be overlooked.

"Present me, Poltimore."

The voice was deep and rich, and almost tragic.

"I beg your pardon, old man. Mr. Alfred Prentice — Miss Chance."

Graham was in the best of spirits. With youth, expectations, and the superabundant health which runs to irresponsibility, how could he be otherwise? "Come, let us go on at once," he shouted in his light-hearted way.

As they walked down to the quay, he looked gladly down at the girl he loved and at last had won, and burst out in rapid eulogy of his new-found friend.

"You will like Prentice, Charity," he cried with enthusiasm. "He is not exactly a Hercules, but he's a very good fellow — and clever, very clever indeed. Just the sort of literary chap you will like to talk to. I fell across him this morning sitting upon the wall at the end of the jetty. I asked him what he was doing. He said he was busy. Incubating a poem, I told him. We were at school together, but he is older than I. Oh! he's a very good chap. He

did my verses and Greek play for years.
That's why he made such a reputation so
young in life. He got the learning meant
for me, in addition to his own. Those
verses he read just now really belonged to
me. He did them vicariously, you know."

Then he laughed, in his light-hearted
way. Now that she had promised to marry
him, he had not a care in the world.

With quickened curiosity the girl glanced
again at the stranger. He was striding
along by the side of Theodosia, apparently
rapt in thought. But then, as Charity
asked herself, how could a man of genius
talk to Theodosia? Inadvertently, no
doubt, he had brought away the little red
volume, and carried it, a finger between
the leaves. Would it surprise him, she
wondered, when he found this out? And
would he read again? She hoped that he
would read again.

"He seems so self-conscious," she said,
almost to herself.

"Don't be prejudiced against him, there's
a dear," whispered Graham, in her ear, for

they were now upon the steps in the quay
side.   It was easy to him to like people,
and Charity was always so critical.   "There
is generally something odd about these
poets.   But they can't help it, you know.
Prentice is a man of deep feeling, — of
really fine feeling.   I want you to like him.
I have asked him to stay with us.   Let me
help you.   Step upon the seat."

A boat was already waiting for them.   A
flash of oars upon the silent harbour.   Then
the rattle of a block as the foresail was run
up, and the "Halcyon" filled her white
wings and stood up the channel, close under
the cliffs.

The wind was scarcely enough to make
the ship heel, although at first she moved
through the water briskly enough.   The girl
leaned back in her chair and looked up into
the clear summer sky.

Graham was lying on the deck beside her.
The others, with the humorous consideration due to lovers newly betrothed, had left
them to themselves, but for a long while
they did not talk.

From a sharp rock, jutting out of the
water, a seagull rose and slowly wheeled
over the passing cutter.   How beautiful it
was!   She could see each feather, as it
hung for a moment just above the mast.
Everything was sweet and calm, and lulled
her soul into contentment.   For the first
time since her engagement, she fully acqui-
esced in her own happiness.   For Aunt
Helen was so happy.   Graham was so
happy.   And yes, she was happy too.

He raised his finger and slowly followed
the bird as it circled overhead, as if he had
been pointing at it with a gun.

"I should hate you if you could kill it,"
she cried, suddenly raising her head to look
at him.   "Could you kill it?"

"Not on those terms," he laughed.

The gull uttered its shrill note, dropped
astern, and settled again upon the rock.
But all her restlessness had returned.   There
was never an escape from her own sensibility when a sight, a sound, or even the
cadence of a word could awaken all the
vague longings of her heart.

"They build upon the ledges of the cliff — and jackdaws in the crevices too. I used to creep along at low tide and pick up the young birds. They get tired and drop when they first begin to fly. Once I stayed too long. You see the slope where it is not quite so steep? I had to climb up there. Half-way up I got stuck. But there was no going back. I had to go on, and I did."

The girl glanced at the dizzy height, with its meagre foothold, and shuddered.

For a moment she was silent; then she spoke with animation: "You had to go on, and you did. That expresses it exactly, Graham. If you had to go on — you would."

"What a moralist you are, Charity!" he told her, with half-amused indolence. "From reading so much poetry with Aunt Helen, you expect every man to be a hero."

Her eyes sparkled, and the colour rose upon her cheek. "I could worship a man who did something," she cried.

"What?"

"No matter what."

Startled at the feeling into which she had been betrayed, and for a moment disconcerted, she again leaned back and looked up at the cliffs. The tide was running faster now, and made a gurgling sound against the cutter's side. Above it they could hear the distant voice of Mrs. Mortimer, in earnest discussion with Mrs. Poltimore-Briggs: "Yes, of the palest apricot, cut very full indeed, and interlined of course with crin —"

"Listen to the words of wisdom, Charity," he whispered, with his imperturbable good-humour.

"Oh, I hate it!" And she clenched her hands and quivered with nervous excitement. "Always the same — the same — the same. Except when they talk of each other, and that's worse. One would suppose there was nothing to think about, and nothing to feel. And it is all so weak and insipid. It isn't living. There is no interest in it. It is like sailing when there is no wind. That always makes me long for a storm. I've been watching the rocks now, and we haven't gone five yards in five minutes. I wish it would blow a hurricane — and carry us over to Wales — so that we had to beat back in the dead of night — in the teeth of a driving rain — with all of them as wet as drowned rats, and afraid too. That would be sailing."

"You would be just as wet as the rest."

"I shouldn't care. I can picture it. Hailstones have beaten down Mrs. Mortimer's back hair. She cannot turn her face to the gale, and one long, tapering lock clings round her neck like damp sea-weed. The unsuspected frame is revealed to the eyes of man. And her artificial set shakes and chatters until the front teeth fall out. Then I hold on tight and am glad in my heart."

Their eyes met, and they burst out laughing. Whatever its intensity, her ill-humour was short-lived, and died in whimsicality. But it left her glowing with animation, and to Graham she had never looked more beautiful.

"What an emotional girl you are, Charity!"

"Oh! I don't know what I am," she said quickly. "Aunt Helen would never tell me. When she took me, I became hers, she said. Do you know, Graham?"

"No," he hesitated.

"But do you know?" she insisted with increasing eagerness.

He paused. "Truly, I do not know, Charity," he told her.

"Sometimes I believe that I am a different animal to the rest of them, and that they resent it, too. That's common in the animal kingdom, you know. Oh, you haven't the least idea what you have undertaken to marry, Graham."

"We have known each other long enough."

"You don't know me a bit," she cried with decision. "They all come and congratulate me now, of course, — even Theodosia. But I know what they say to each other. They surmise what Aunt Helen has to leave you, and what you'll get from your

father, and then they say, ' Charity Chance
has done well for herself.' They hate me
for that. I don't care, only it is all so
mean; and it's not true. I could love
you ten **times** as much if all of a sudden you had n't a penny, and we had to
begin in a house the size of a hutch —
and struggle on — and fight it all out —
and watch it all grow up. That would be
living!"

With growing enthusiasm her voice had
risen, and she stopped, as if fearing to be
overheard. But Mrs. Mortimer had been
to a flower-show the day before, and her
store of interesting information was inexhaustible.

"A blouse of a medium shade of green,
accordion-kilted chiffon, with sleeves of
cream and pink *chiné* silk, green satin
ribbon at the waist, carried three parts of
the way up the figure — "

Then the boom came home, and this
excellent woman ducked her head.

"You ought to go and talk to them!"
urged Charity. "There is Mr. Prentice

receiving none of the attention he deserves and longs for."

"He's all right," replied Graham, with a glance at the empty sail. "Besides, there's plenty of time. The wind has dropped and we sha'n't get home for hours unless it freshens. I'll break it to them and come back."

The wind did not freshen. The sun sank behind a sea as smooth as glass, and the grey night crept along the cliffs and wrapt the rocks in gloom. The "Halcyon" drifted slowly homewards on the tide. The girl stood with her hand upon the stay, and watched the stars peer clearer and clearer through the darkening sky. It was all so unspeakably beautiful and deep with mystery that she could scarcely keep from tears. The women were cackling about being so late, but she did not hear them. Graham had spoken more than once, but she did not reply.

"We shall have to tow her in," he said. "I'll get in the boat and take an oar."

The boat was brought alongside. He

stepped into her, and Charity was left alone.

To the creaking of the oars against the rowlocks, they slowly glided into the harbour mouth.

It was quite late. The lights of Babblemouth were mostly in the upper windows, and long reflections fell in shimmering lines across the black water below the quay. Charity sighed. The gloom of the harbour was so much sadder than the pale starlight of the open sea.

"Every candle there is the beacon of a tragedy."

She started. Unobserved, Alfred Prentice had stepped upon the deck, and was standing where Graham had just now stood.

"You quite frightened me," she gasped. "I did not know any one was near. But surely that is not so. It would be terrible to think that people are not happy."

"Only the unimportant is happy."

Certainly no gaiety detracted from the importance of Mr. Alfred Prentice. He was oracular out of the profoundest depths of sad experience.

The words made a deep impression upon
the girl's mind; but before she could firmly
grasp them to reply, the moment had come
to go ashore. Upon the quay the party
quickly dispersed. It was too late to loiter,
and Graham walked home with her at once.
But along the road she was silent. "Only
the unimportant is happy." The phrase
haunted her. Yet she could not get hold
of it. It was shadowy and illusive — this
ghost of a great truth. "Only the unimportant is happy." Of course! people who
were satisfied with trivialities could get
them, — they were common as blackberries,
in all conscience. But "only the unimportant" — that was so sad.

A touch of sadness could always fire this
girl's sympathy, which, once aglow, must
needs shine on the nearest object.

"I have been quite horrid to you to-night,
Graham. I know I have," she confessed,
as they stepped under the porch.

Then she put her hands upon his shoulders and raised her face to his.

"Not at all, Charity. You have been delightful, as you always are," he cried in rapture.

It was the first time she had kissed him of her own free will.

CHAPTER VII.

THE PLEACHÈD BOWER.

THE wicket-gate at the end of the shrubbery path opened into a ride through a small larch plantation, whence a broken footpath meandered up the coombe-side to the top of the wood. The way was steep and rugged. In places huge boulders of smooth blue rock, hidden from below by overspreading branches, stood boldly out from the hill.

Upon the crest of one of these promontories a leaning ash formed a natural and unsuspected bower. But for years the place had been known to Charity.

In early childhood, no sooner was she free of the wood than this wild crag captivated her imagination. It was the background of all her dreams: the scene in

which was re-enacted every story she knew.
And Charity's childhood had been brought
up on stories of the best; for the little cripple to whom fable was more real than fact,
fascinated by the open-eyed wonder of the
child, would go on and on for hours. Thus
the place became by turns a bandit's castle,
the Tarpeian rock, and the cave of Poly-
pheme. And it was all her own; for either
Graham had not heard the stories, or from
a tree-top looked down with lordly contempt upon such make-believes.

This haunt had never lost its charm.
The fading visions of childish fancy were
replaced by a keen sense of the natural
beauty of the nook. There Charity spent
many a summer hour, and no one ever came.
The casual trespasser wandered heedless
by. Unaware that he was watched, the
village boy ran through the wood below,
and stopped to peer into the trees for nests.
And this inviolable secrecy made of this
bower a sanctuary to which the girl fled
when pursued by the spirit of her own
restlessness.

There also she often went to work.   The
evening readings with Miss Graham, although they sometimes lasted deep into
the night, could not satisfy her passion for
poetry and fiction.   And there was no
dearth of books, besides, for strange volumes
from the library of the late Dr. Graham,
sleeping in one of the disused rooms of
Babblemouth House, found their way into
the hands of Charity Chance.

Moreover, she was writing a tale, and
had been for a long time: a story of village
life, which made little progress because she
never could satisfy herself with what was
done.   In the room above the porch, at
night when all was still, in an ecstasy of
excitement and delight she would write
pages.   It was beautiful.   She could see
it — feel it all — and, read by the pale lamp-
light, it filled her eyes with tears.   She lay
awake with gladness to dream it over again.
But in the morning, in the calm solitude of
her retreat, everything was changed.   The
freshness had faded; the sweetness was
gone.   It was no better than the flower

plucked yesterday and withered in an hour.
Sometimes it seemed impossible that a
thing wrought with such emotion could be
so poor. Then in despair she cast it aside
and did no more for weeks.

Yet the hope never forsook her heart.
To the child of her imagination she must
at last return. And meanwhile she watched
eagerly to catch the soul of humble country
life, and the quaint ways of it, which looked
so much like humours and were not.

Amongst other things, she collected the
sayings of John Sprake.

Already they covered reams, those similes
bequeathed from an old world where no man
might be merely bald, but "so bald as a
bladder o' lard," and nothing crooked was
allowed to be less crooked than "a dog's
hind leg." The furniture of John's brain
had been in his family for generations.

After the sail some days elapsed before
she again met Mr. Prentice. He mooned
away by himself along the cliffs, Graham
told her with a laugh. She could understand
that. He had need of solitude to mature

his great thoughts. But even to have spoken to a poet reawakened all her longings and aspirations. Again the neglected manuscript saw the light, and she carried it that morning with her into the wood.

The summer weather remained unchanged, and through the still air came quite clearly the talk and laughter of haymakers in the meadows across the coombe. "Captain-ah, Whoa!" called the boy to his horses as they moved the load. In one of the great oaks above a wood-pigeon kept cooing all the time.

There came a footstep in the wood. She raised her head to listen, but she did not look. What could it matter to her who passed that way? She was secure from interruption in her retreat, and with impatience she turned again to the closely written sheet.

Suddenly from below came the voice of Jan Sprake raised in high expostulation.

"There idden no vootpath thik way, zir. You can't go 'long there no ways 't all. I 've agot my orders zo clear as the day,

to turn everybeddy back out o' theäs wood.
Gentle or simple, back they've agot to go,
sure as a gun. There idden no two ways
'bout it. 'T is so much as my life's wo'th
if Squire Poltimore-Briggs were to zee.
He'd rear the place. I have agot to be
kep' zo quiet as the grave — 'bout the pheasants, you see, zir."

From the height of argument Jan's voice
gradually sank into the confidential whisper
of regret. He was such a stickler for duty,
however painful it might be. Charity crept
forward and peered over the brink of the
rock. Jan had taken off his hat, and was
ostentatiously wiping his heated brow with
a red handkerchief. Mr. Prentice stood
looking at him with an evident lack of interest as to whether he went forward or back,
which nothing could disconcert.

"I only came here out of the sun," he
said.

"You zee," Jan went on instructively,
"there's a hen-pheasant — or may be two —
do nest here so reg'lar as the year. An' if
he don't vind 'em, why, Squire Briggs he

do fus about like a vly in a glue-pot. An'
he don't forget to talk loud, nother. But
there, to be sure, a gen'leman like you don'
want to go a-tearen about the wood like a
mad feller — No, no. You thought just to
stalkety roun' like, under the shade o' the
leaf like."

"It is of no consequence. I'll get back
the way I came," interrupted the great man
in his impressive bass, and turned upon his
heel.

"There, you've agot no call to do that,"
said Jan, in a manner suddenly become
coaxing. "There idden a soul 'pon earth
to say a word to ee 'ithout 't is I myzelf, an'
I mus' run back zo shuttle as a rabbit, an'
exercise my ho'ses. Why, you mid walk
here till doomsday an' no man never the
wiser. An' you had no need to zay I've
a-zeed ee. I sha'n't come up to ee no more.
Fags! I be pretty well a-sweltered, sure
'nough. There, 't is my duty to come up,
fear 't is some poachen feller, look-y-zee.
There, vor my part, I do often wish to God
there were no pheasants, e'ens 's mid zay.

For 'tis wo'th a shillen to come up here. Zo 't is. 'Pon my life 't is."

In vain he dramatically mopped his head, for the retiring trespasser did not turn round.

. " All a shillen," reflected Jan Sprake, with deep conviction.

But there was no response.

" An' more too," he growled with growing discontent.

" This gentleman is a friend of Mr. Poltimore, John."

Jan was startled. The voice, familiar but indignant, came out of the clouds. As he explained later on, when subsequent proceedings had rendered even this small incident of public interest, he was that " tookt aback" that he turned " so white as a hound's tooth." He looked all ways to once. An' there, sure enough, were Miss Charity a-stood 'pon top o' the rock so bold as a statute.

But Jan thought nothing of this at the time. He only muttered an apology, that he saw the gen'leman wur a gen'leman so

soon as ever he clapped eyes 'pon un, and
if it had n' a-bin for his duty he would n'
a-wored out shoe-leather to a-comed up.
Then he turned away and went thought-
fully home to the house.

Alfred Prentice caught a glimpse of a
pale summer frock disappearing amongst
the leaves. Then Charity came hurrying
down the wood to him.

She felt ashamed, and, in anxiety to prove
him welcome, spoke with warmth, almost
with emotion. "Please do not go away,
Mr. Prentice. I am quite sure Miss Graham
would be vexed beyond measure. The foolish man has been here so long that he be-
lieves the place his, and acts entirely without authority. And as to pheasants, — there
are no pheasants. There was one once,
but, rest his soul! he's dead. You are
more likely, it appears, to meet with a beast
of prey."

"Or a Dryad, perhaps," he suggested
solemnly. Then noticing the roll of papers
in her hand, he added: "But you were at
work, and I have interrupted you." He

appeared pained. His brow contracted with sympathetic grief, and his voice quite quavered with regret. It seemed to say: "Too well I know myself these terrible encroachments upon the solitude of the soul."

She hastened to reassure him. "Oh! I only amuse myself. I like to go up under the trees out of sight and sit alone. I have found a place where no one ever comes."

"Show me such a place," he said quite softly, and sighed.

Was this affectation? Or merely the manner natural to a spirit very delicately strung? As she led the way between the gnarled trunks and under the twisted branches of the oaks, she kept asking herself this question. For what was affectation in another might be quite natural to a poet.

They reached the top of the rock. Half hidden by brake and undergrowth lay a slanting slab of stone, and without ceremony he sat down upon it. He took off his hat, and passed his hand over his long black hair, but for a while he did not speak. The house, the mill, and the cottages below looked like toys, and from this height the distant line of the blue sea came almost level with the brim of the cliffs.

"Those are the happy people," he said, pointing down at the haymakers. "They understand each other and are understood. Their life is full of light and laughter. They are never alone. They never seek a place where no one comes."

He spoke with deep melancholy, in pity mostly for himself, but partly for a people so supremely happy.

"I am glad to have met you again, Mr. Prentice," said the girl, warmly. "Something you said the other night impressed me deeply. I was afraid you might be going. Do you remember saying that in every house is some great tragedy? That may be, perhaps, and people keep their deeper troubles hidden. But it seems to me that into every life comes a great sorrow. Now these people that you speak of — I know them all — every one. They are too simple to hide a trouble. They seem to want to tell it to get relief. That tall woman, for instance, raking apart by herself is a widow. Only last week she lost her son, killed in a colliery in Wales. And he was so good to her too."

The girl spoke in deep earnest; and the last phrase as she uttered it was rich with sympathy and regret. He scarcely glanced at the lonely figure in the field, for already, whilst Charity was speaking, he had drifted into reverie. The cadence of that sentence recalled his attention. Not the real sorrow of the woman, so much as the sound of Charity's voice, touched his sensibilities. The emotion of the girl was more powerful to move him than the story itself, which indeed he could not have correctly told. "And he was so good to her too." She was standing on the edge of the rock, and when he looked up, there was at least a moisture in his eyes. Had she spoken ten words more, he would have been in tears.

What a heart this man has! thought Charity. She felt humiliated to remember that at first she had accused him of affectation.

He began to talk, quickly and with growing excitement.

"Yes," he sighed, "there is always a deep sorrow. But the griefs that are common to humanity are understood of all mankind. Death comes, and people flock with flowers to hide the barren blackness of the bier. Even strangers lay a cool sweet leaf upon the wound, and soon there remains nothing but a scar, at last forgotten if it be not rudely touched. But who can minister to the unknown sorrows of the mind? The lost illusion, who shall replace it? Or who lay the haunting memory of a dead hope?"

He paused, and looked away across the sea.

"But surely —" She hesitated. His words moved her to compassion, they sounded so real, and she felt shy of seeming not to understand. "Surely it is better to outlive an illusion. That is — well — one step towards truth. And to bury a hope is not despair. Other hopes spring up."

She stopped abruptly. He had fixed his eyes upon her, and she was disconcerted. Her halting sentences could go no further.

"I am glad I wandered this way. From the first moment I saw you at Poltimore's I wanted to talk to you," he went on, speaking quite intimately, as if he had known her for years. "The other people had been bothering me — making me read and that sort of thing. But I knew that you were sympathetic. I felt it would be a precious privilege to know you. And they had been saying you were so fond of poetry. Ah — Have you read me?"

Very little, she was forced to confess.

"Do you come here every day?"

"Oh, no. Only occasionally."

"To-morrow?"

"I never know beforehand. I must go. I see Miss Graham in the garden. She will want me."

"Come to-morrow," he whispered; "and if you will permit me I should like to bring you my poor book. What there is of me is in it."

She thanked him heartily in her frank girlish way. "I am quite sure it is beautiful," she said; and having hastily shaken hands, she hurried down the hill.

She came into the garden glowing with excitement and delight. Her imagination was on fire. She had talked of something deeper than the babble and trivialities of Babblemouth. And from what a depth of sympathy and understanding he had spoken! He indeed must have suffered some great sorrow, — she could feel that in every word he uttered.

Miss Graham was sitting in the bath-chair on the lawn.

"Why, Charity, what a colour you have, child! I feel the wind here. Push me down to the drooping ash. Where have you been?"

"In the wood; I met Mr. Prentice, and had quite a talk with him. Graham's friend, you know, — the poet."

"Poet!" flashed out the shrewd little lady, with an impatient wave of the hand. "That's not a poet. I have seen him on

the road several times, but to look at him
once is quite enough. No, dear, I have
met men of genius, in years gone by. Some
of them had odd ways, but underneath all
was real — soul, or passion, or a great heart,
with only a thin shell of folly. But there
is nothing real about that person — except
the affectation. A little farther, dear.
There. Stop."

The girl's face was out of sight behind
the creases of the leather hood, and her
impulse to make quick reply passed unobserved of those keen grey eyes. She too
had harboured a like prejudice, and she
longed to contradict — to set this false impression right. But there were moments of
rapid nervous perception, when Miss Graham could not brook even a difference of
opinion. And she had spoken with such
emphatic, clear decision. The moment
passed, and Charity remained silent. She
had been on the verge of speaking of to-
morrow and the expected book. But that
was not possible now, and the words died
on her lips. Yet she felt mean, to find she

had not courage to defend this man who had already interested her so much.   And for the first time in her life she was not altogether frank with the woman whose tenderness had befriended her for more years than memory could look back.

CHAPTER VIII.

EVERMORE TATTLING.

FROM that moment of reticence a new and growing unrest began to trouble the soul of Charity Chance. The finer instinct, which stirred her indignation against the Babblemouth folk, and made her writhe under their littleness, turned upon itself. Hitherto no stain of conscious meanness had ever sullied her self-respect. Slights, like pruning, only forced her pride into stronger growth. She had never known anything to hide, nor to fear, nor to reproach herself with.

But on the following day she waited until Miss Graham was busy with her letters, and watched Jan Sprake into the stable, before going into the wood. To avoid the

open path she climbed the hill under cover
of the trees. The book, which was quite
small, she brought home in her pocket, and
read throughout the night in the little
chamber above the porch.

Some of the verses were love-songs, and
they had a deeper reality because she knew
the man who wrote them. Line after line
she read and re-read aloud, and in the still-
ness every word spoke to her. They filled
her brain with excitement, they set her
heart on fire. In the glow of it her imagination shaped fantastic stories of the hopeless
love of Alfred Prentice. He was so sad and
melancholy — and again to-day he had talked
of loneliness and sympathy. He had loved
— and lost. Not dead, but faithless, the
maiden who had wrecked his life. Fallen
away, because she could not understand.
This dream was so vivid that it imprinted
itself upon Charity's mind like fact. She
pitied him from the bottom of her heart.

One poem she could not comprehend.
The words were magnificent, and the sound
almost sublime, but the sense was illusive,

and escaped her again and again. If she
might only hear it read, she thought, she
could catch the meaning. And he had
begged her to meet him again. To give
him frankly her opinion upon his poor trifles,
he said.

She had not promised, but the desire to
go became irresistible. After all she was
but following the habit of her leisure in
going into the wood. There was no harm
in talking to a friend of the man to whom
she was engaged. Yet she felt with disgust
that these unsuspected interviews more and
more engrossed her thoughts. And to
Graham she had not mentioned Alfred
Prentice's name. "You have chosen the
one to me the most precious," sighed the
poet, and read, as he assured her, with the
greatest pleasure. She was too shy to ask
him what it meant.

So the days passed on. Prentice still
remained in Babblemouth, lodging in one
of the little houses looking down upon the
quay. But when the first glory of the rising celebrity faded in the commonplace light

of familiar day, there was no end to the criticisms of the Babblemouth folk. They sneered at his loitering ways, and laughed at the length of his hair. "But then, there is always something odd," said Theodosia, "about people who are supposed to be clever."

Such little disparagements stung Charity to the quick. Retorts came upon the tip of her tongue, but she could not trust herself to utter them. Within her heart smouldered an anger she dared not disclose. A breath must blow it into flame. Yet how ungenerous to remain silent and hear a higher intelligence attacked by fools! It was hard to contain herself, yet harder still to contemplate her own cowardice.

There comes at last a moment when the bow snaps.

They had come over to Babblecombe one afternoon, these Babblemouth people. There was tea by the corner of the lawn, and Graham was handing round the bread-and-butter. The unwillingness of Mr. Poltimore-Briggs to stand for Parliament had been fully discussed. His reluctant yielding to over-whelming persuasion in spite of her entrea-ties, Mrs. Poltimore-Briggs had dramatically described.

"It was no good for me to say anything, my dear," she assured Miss Graham; "none whatever. His Lordship met him and said, 'You'd better stand, Poltimore.' His Lordship always forgets and calls him Poltimore, you know. 'You'd better stand, and do your best to push out the Radical.' So he consented." Then she threw up her hands in despair.

"Talking of Radicals," cried Mrs. Mortimer, stopping at every few words to dip her beak into the tea-cup. "The Rector says — though of course he would not have it repeated for the world as coming from him — that Mr. Prentice is an awful Radical. Doesn't believe in God — nor in Queen Victoria — nor tithes. Well! I think any man who would rob a church doesn't deserve to live. But I never thought he looked quite a gentleman."

"What is he doing here?" asked Miss

Graham, carelessly. "Charity fell across
him the other day in the wood. Did n't
you say so, Charity?"

But before the girl could answer, Mrs.
Poltimore-Briggs had started again.

"My dear, that is just the way he wanders about. No doubt he thinks the wood
is his. The poetic imagination knows no
bounds, you know. Oh, I don't know what
he is doing here. We asked him to come
to us, but he told Graham he would rather
be free. We did n't want him, of course.
We thought it would be only civil, as he
used to be a friend of Graham. But since
he prefers the freedom of old mother Dibbin's two stuffy little rooms — well, so
much the better. What was that she said
to you, Theodosia? You told me the other
day."

Theodosia shone with the pride of pro-
prietary information.

"Oh, that was nothing! I believe she
was in doubt about her rent. She only said
she supposed it was all right, as he was a
friend of Mr. Poltimore-Briggs, but she

never took in anybody before with such a few things. No more cloth clothes than what he stood upright in, and only three shirts to his back."

"Then no doubt you pointed out to her the impertinence of talking about the private affairs of other people."

The shaft was sudden and unexpected. The hot blood rushed to the cheek of the wounded Theodosia, and Mrs. Poltimore-Briggs was reduced to silence and astonishment. Beside the small round table, brought from the drawing-room for the occasion, stood Charity, contemptuous and defiant, clutching a china tea-pot in her hand.

"Charity! Charity dear!" murmured in remonstrance little Miss Graham; but her lips were twitching with suppressed amusement.

"I think three sufficient for Prentice," cried Graham, with an air of grave deliberation. He had thrown himself upon the grass, and was enjoying well-merited rest after overwhelming exertions. "You see,

he does n't ride 'em so very hard. He lies
in bed by day, and sits up at night in a red
damask dressing-gown awaiting the rosy-
footed dawn. The early morning chills the
imagination. The best inspiration comes
with a smell of paraffin. It is all tommy-
rot about Nature. These chaps only know
the names of things. Prentice can't tell
an ash from an Arbele poplar. I'd bet two
to one whenever the leaves turn up white in
the wind he thinks it's a willow. He
makes up a Nature of his own in bed with
the blind drawn down. I went to look him
up the other afternoon. They said he
was n't down yet, and I ran up and rapped
at his bedroom door. 'Who's there, what
do you want?' responded a voice muffled
with counterpane. 'Are you ill, Prentice?'
I said. 'Shall I come in?' There was a
brief pause whilst he struggled free of the
counterpane. 'Go 'way, go 'way,' he
yelled; 'I'm busy.'"

Charity did not join in the laughter which
followed. She did not take the tale for
truth, but only as one of Graham's irrespon-

sible stories, and she was vexed that he
had not sided with her.

"But I thought you liked him," she cried
with eagerness.

"So I did," he admitted. "But I can't
stand him now."

"Or understand," she retorted, quick as
thought.

No wonder that Charity Chance was not
universally beloved. But Graham loved her
with all his heart, and it was in admiration
that he whispered as he rose to his feet:
"I believe you see the frivolities of everybody you know, and believe in the virtues
of everybody you don't know." His tenderness touched her.

"But you are not going yet, Graham?"

"The Governor has an open-air meeting
on the down, and I must walk over to it.
Come to the top of the hill, Charity," he
begged.

So they presently went together, side by
side, up the white dusty road. "She is so
high-minded, and he has such a good heart,"
thought the little cripple as her eyes fol-

lowed them every step of the way. "They were made for each other," she said to herself. And indeed it looked so as they slowly passed out of sight on the hill-top.

CHAPTER IX.

IN THE WOOD.

No matter if she were late. Aunt Helen would not mind in the least. And the Babblemouth people would stay. Oh yes! The Babblemouth people would be pleased to stay. So Charity walked some distance with Graham, being willing to make amends. When at last she got back to the hill-top, the sun was glowing red through a belt of grey mist over the sea; a hawk was hovering high above the cliff.

She stood upon the ridge awhile to rest, a solitary figure in bold relief against the sky. The people on the lawn saw and discussed as to whether it were she. Theodosia thought the person far too tall.

The embers of resentment were still burning within her heart. What a little world where people were so ready to belittle everybody! And she had promised to spend her life in this coombe, — this tea-cup. Ever the same dreary little round, with no true sympathy, no understanding. She thought a great deal about true sympathy since Alfred Prentice once used the words.

Of late, also, a question kept arising in her mind to which no answer could possibly be found. It lived with her by day, it haunted her by night. It tormented her like a lost word. Whence had she been brought here? To whom had she belonged in nature and in love? who nevertheless parted with her without a pang. For surely they might at least have longed to watch over her welfare. It flashed across her mind that out of jealousy of possession Miss Graham had prevented all communication. "You were mine," she had told her, "after I took you." In a moment of passionate yearning the girl cried out that she had been robbed, — that nothing could recompense for the love implanted by Nature which must have filled her life. Then she burst into tears of contrition at her own ingratitude.

These moods of vague restlessness had become very common with her of late.

In the courtyard below still remained the carriage of Mrs. Poltimore-Briggs. The presence of that exemplary woman relieved Charity from haste. A footpath, little used, ran along the hill around the brim of the coombe. After the dry road the grass was soft and cool, and the girl walked on towards the wood.

She came upon two rustic lovers loitering by a stile, too absorbed in themselves and each other to hear her coming footsteps on the turf. In uncouth fashion the youth's arm encircled the girl's waist. To let Charity pass, they started back, happy, blushing, conscious, but complete. "Yes, these are the happy people," she said to herself; "they understand each other and are understood."

But Graham would never understand *her*.

Already the engagement began to oppress her soul. Why should she marry? She did not want to marry. She would rather go into the world, and fight, and earn her living, and be free. Those people who gave her up must have been poor and afraid. Fools! She would have worked for them. No, no! They were good, and out of tenderness desired for her more than they had to give.

No sunshine fell upon the trees to-night. The distant haze drank up the glory of the light, and the leaden sea melted and was lost in violet cloud. By the time Charity reached the wood, beneath the heavy branches it was growing dusk. It must be later than she had thought. Something moved, and a pigeon flew from the ivy close beside her. She quickened her pace for fear of being overtaken by the darkness.

"Miss Chance!"

The voice startled her. She knew it well, and it made her heart beat fast. She had not thought of meeting him to-night, and a strange fear fell upon her — of what she knew not. She must not stay. Yet at the sound of her name she stopped.

She heard him hurrying down the hillside. A loose stone came rolling amongst the briers by her feet, and in his haste he stumbled over an uncovered twisted root.

"I was sure I should meet you," he stammered, still breathless from his effort to recover himself. "The idea got hold of me so that I was compelled to come. It was an inspiration."

"I am just going in," she replied quickly, for his eager manner heightened her agitation; then she turned to continue on her way.

"Not for a few minutes, pray. And I will walk down with you to the fir copse. Let me help you, Charity. I may say Charity here in the twilight, may I not? Give me your hand; the gloom of the trees makes it so dark."

She could not refuse, and he helped her over the broken stones and out-cropping rock.

"We have had so many talks here in the

wood, and my mind was full of you. I
could think of nothing else. You became
a necessity to me. Then I came out here
where the very leaves whisper of you. Besides, I knew you would come. It was
inevitable."

She was not superstitious; but his words
were full of passion, and so deep with conviction that they overawed her, like the
utterances of an oracle unfolding unalterable
destiny. They had reached an open space
where sticks of felled timber were lying on
the ground. She tried to withdraw her
hand, but he held it fast.

"I must go. I must go at once. I cannot stay," she implored.

"For one moment you must listen to me,
Charity — "

"I cannot listen. I am not free to
listen."

In her anxiety and helplessness the words
sounded like a lament.

"I cannot help it," he whispered. "No
power on earth shall prevent my saying I
love you. From the first moment I was

certain of your sympathy. I could see in every movement the quickness of your sensibilities. And the world is so dead and dull. They had been making me read, but what did they care for my verses? What does anybody care? I had ceased to care myself. But you quickened me into new hope — new aspiration. Every syllable you spoke was like the touch of a human hand."

He was so moved at this his own picture of sympathy that his voice faltered, and he stopped.

Each word went red-hot to the girl's heart. It had come, the thing she thought impossible, — the love they spoke of as irresistible, which she had never felt. Every element that in imagination went to the making of an ideal passion was present. He was exceptional. He had heart, intellect, soul. And he had need of her, — deep spiritual need.

A flame of sudden joy leapt up within her bosom. Then again she was afraid, and her reply was angry in self-defence, —

"I — I am sorry to hear you speak like

this, Mr. Prentice.   You — you hurt me.   I
have liked, yes, really liked talking to you
— and in future I — you have made it
impossible — "

"I know.   That is the tale they always
teach," he cried bitterly.   "If your heart
has an impulse, hide it.   If it cherish an
emotion, crush it.   They are afraid of their
lives to live, and that is the gospel in which
they bring you up.   Because I love you,
you must refuse even to speak to me, — even
though you be necessary to me.   And that
is the wisdom of the world."

As he finished, his voice sank into its
habitual melancholy, and he released her
hand.   Her brain was whirling in its effort
to seize his deepest meaning.   For he
seemed to say so much whilst she could
grasp so little.   And all that stood clear
out of the chaos was himself, a lonely figure
with the world arrayed against him, crav-
ing for sympathy and help.

"I should have to think whether it was
right," she said very softly, as if speaking
to herself.

His manner changed. He spoke with a subdued tenderness, a really touching self-restraint, —

"Yes. I recognise that as an inevitable necessity of your nature. To me, everything that is real is right."

"I meant really right. Not what people think," she hastily explained.

Something rustled past them amongst the ferns and undergrowth, and she involuntarily started aside.

"It was nothing," he assured her. "I fancy a rabbit flitted across by the felled tree."

"I must go."

"One moment, Charity."

But the movement had disturbed her, and regardless of his entreaty she walked quickly on.

In places the rough pathway was too narrow for two to pass, and he followed until they came to the open ride between the larches. By this time it was nearly dark. She stopped abruptly and held out her hand.

"Good-bye, Mr. Prentice."

"I have only one thing to ask," he pleaded wildly. "My love has startled you. How could I help it? You have come into my life. You have become part of me. Could I stifle a generous passion at its birth, and bury it out of sight like a crime? Believe me, life knows too little love to lightly cast it aside. I cannot do so. You cannot. And you tell me the hours when we have met were precious to you. Come once more to-morrow. Come with this knowledge in your heart and talk to me again. That is all I ask. Just once."

She did not promise him. Before she could make up her mind, a tall figure came into the ride, striding rapidly towards them. It was already quite dark.

"Some one is here," she whispered in alarm. "Good-night."

"Morning, noon, or evening, I shall wait until you come."

And so they parted. He disappeared amongst the larches, and she turned quietly towards the house.

By the wicket-gate she was overtaken by Theodosia.

"Why, Charity, is that you?" cried she, in great surprise. "I went up to look for foxgloves, and found a few. Come along, you shall shield me from a row. Look!" and she held out the bunch of flowers in the dusk.

They hurried to the house in silence. For Charity's tongue clove to the roof of her mouth, and her brain kept throbbing with the thought, It has come — it has come!

CHAPTER X.

HONITON LACE.

"To me the thing that is real is right."

How his phrases haunted her, and this more than any. She pondered over it, perplexed. Ever and again it arose before her mind, boldly claiming acceptance as a universal truth. The envy of those Babblemouth people was real enough, but reality did not make it right. Within the converse, rather, Truth lay cradled. "The thing that is unreal is wrong." Unconsciously she substituted this proposition, and cherished the changeling unawares. "What depth of insight he has!" she gasped, and almost worshipped him for the thing he had not said.

She did not go to meet Prentice the next day. She trembled at the thought. She had promised to marry Graham. Her path was plain before her, and she must keep to it.

In the isolation of her growing up, as the fairest flower in Miss Graham's garden, she had seen nothing of the outside world. Lessons she had learned in the Babblemouth High School, an institution of considerable local repute, but her real education went forward at home. There she drank deep in poetry, the wine of the little cripple's life, until her whole soul throbbed and glowed with high ideals. Now amongst these a deadly strife had arisen.

She had promised to marry Graham. Constancy was a virtue beyond compare, and she must keep her word. But how could she longer acquiesce in his love, and act the lie her lips would never deign to utter?

In her distress and misery she would creep away to her room over the porch, or to some odd corner of the garden, to be with her own thoughts unseen. For she could not hide her agitation. And she dared not tell it to any one. In solitude it was a relief to speak her heart aloud; and she poured out her secret passion to the tall sunflowers beside the garden wall.

"It has come. I love him!" she cried. "I love him with all my heart." Then she stood silent, startled at the vehemence of her own utterances.

She must never speak to him again: that was the only way. But this resolution brought a burden of despair, beneath which her spirit was well-nigh broken.

So the days passed on. A doubt whether Theodosia had seen them together that night, which at first troubled her, was dismissed. She had not spoken of it. But a rumour of impending dissolution had given a keener interest to the candidature of Mr. Poltimore-Briggs, and the Babblemouth people could talk of nothing else. There were meetings all over the country. To-morrow there was to be a mass meeting on the quay. And Graham had thrown himself into the contest heart and soul, — not from any deep conviction, but with the

careless gaiety of the sportsman. Therefore, of him, for the time, she saw but
little. Miss Graham, noticing the girl's unhappiness, but mistaking its cause, became
more than ever tender and sympathetic.

"Lay aside the book, and talk to me,"
she said softly one evening, and gently
drew the girl down to kiss her bright hair.
"You must not mind, dear, if he seems to
neglect you, just for a while. There is
nowhere a more loyal heart than Graham.
Why, I would not care for him one straw,
if he were not eager for his father to win.
He would not be worth his salt. And no
one could love you better, Charity dear, in
all the world."

The little lady stopped. There were
tears in her eyes, but they were tears of
happiness. For the girl's melancholy was
a source of joy, since it proved the depth of
her affection.

"I know that Graham loves me," replied
Charity in a low voice.

"He worships you," cried Miss Graham,
her face bright with enthusiasm. "Wait

one moment, child. I will be back. No, do not move. I can go alone."

She waved away the proffered assistance, and with only her ebony stick, toiled upstairs. She was gone some time. Charity could hear her mysteriously moving overhead, and that she dragged a box upon the floor. At last she returned, bringing with great care a small flat parcel wrapped in blue paper.

Fatigued and out of breath, without a word she took her seat. Overcome with emotion, for a while she held the precious burden on her lap. Then with a quick gesture, beckoned Charity to unfasten the string. The knot, tied long ago, was very firm, and the girl knelt down to pick it out.

With trembling hands, herself, she opened the paper, and drew forth a wealth of Honiton lace, and amongst it a bridal veil.

"Stay, child, stay!" she interposed quickly, for Charity was about to rise.

She rapidly unfolded the veil, yellow with age and very beautiful, and cast it over the girl's head.

"There, Charity," she began in a broken voice. "My mother wore it at the altar, and so shall you. It was made for her. And the flounce too. For more than a score of years it has not seen the light. Poor Irene put it on once, and laughed to look at herself. She should have worn it, but that was not to be. Stand over there, dear, and let me look at it again."

The girl hesitated, then obeyed. In her effort to control her feelings, she held her head erect, as if in pride.

"Yes, yes. You shall wear it," cried the little cripple, nodding approval. She paused, and then went on with growing excitement: "Charity! You will be a bride for a king. And you shall keep it, dear, as I have done, until some day you put it on a child of your own. For you are mine, dear — and Graham's — and there is no one else. It shall be an heirloom for ever to the first daughter who marries. No. That will be always a fresh name. For the bride of the eldest son."

Suddenly she stopped.

"Come here, child! Quick! Let me take it off."

Her manner had changed, and she spoke now in a frightened whisper.

"They used to call it unlucky to try on a bride's things. They said so when Irene put it on. And she, poor girl — Quick, kneel down again!"

She quickly removed, and was tenderly refolding the precious relic to put it by, when her eye caught sight of the misery upon the girl's face.

"Of course there is nothing in that," she said soothingly. "How foolish of me to have said it, dear!"

Then the little lady laughed uneasily, and again drew the girl towards her to be kissed.

"There. Quick, pick me up the string," she said.

But both the exultation and the passing presentiment had pressed with crushing weight upon Charity's spirit. The one proved the marriage, and the other the unhappiness so inevitable. To hide her emotion she turned away and crossed the room to the piano. She stood, turning over the leaves of a volume of Beethoven's sonatas, but did not touch the keys.

There followed a brief moment of silence and disquietude.

How sensitive she is! thought the little cripple, and loved her the more for it. Then out of kindness she began to prattle quite lightly upon an unimportant matter.

"Your friend the poet, Charity, seems to have betaken himself to the woods. He is there all the day through, so John Sprake tells me, and sometimes after dark. John was greatly concerned as to what he could want there, and thought he could never be quite right. But I told him to leave the poor man in peace. I suppose it is a sort of browsing on Parnassus. I would not rob a poor soul of an inspiration for the world. Play something, dear."

The girl gladly turned to the piano for relief, and for that evening there was no further conversation. She placed the book upon the music-rack, and began to play.

But through the solemn adagio and the
fiercer passion of the presto movement, a
vision of Alfred Prentice, desolate and
alone, wandering in the gloom of a hopeless
love, haunted her imagination. He had
implored her to see him again. Since he
loved her so deeply, did she not owe him
as much as this? to own the happiness of
his love, and then to bravely bow to the
inevitable, and say farewell. Only of him
she thought now; not of herself. It was
the essential quality of all her dreams that
they were noble. They pictured everybody
heroic, never yielding to selfishness or fear.
Except the Babblemouth people, whom,
when they were not present, she dismissed
from her mind. It was cruel to be so
abrupt. If not to-morrow, when the political meeting might interfere, then on the
day following, she must meet him once
more, and make an end of it.

CHAPTER XI.

THE MEETING.

BABBLEMOUTH was astir! True, it was a little place, but, once aroused, it displayed that phenomenal activity which is the brightest attribute of a little body. Villagers flocked in from all around, and filled the town to overflowing. A brass band paraded the streets, and other attractions were manifold. There was to be an orator from a distance, a display of fireworks, and it was rumoured that a tight-rope dancer would walk from cliff to cliff upon a slack wire. Many understood that Mr. Poltimore-Briggs hmself would perform this feat, but the event proved this a mere Radical invention.

Below Mr. Poltimore-Briggs's mansion, and running parallel with the harbour, was a row of ancient houses, quaint and irregu-

lar. Between them and the quay lay an
open space, where fishing-boats put up their
spoil to auction, and country-folk pitched
their wares on market day. Upon this
forum a wooden platform had been raised
with seats to accommodate a hundred supporters. There Mr. Poltimore-Briggs was
to address the electorate.

It was evening. The proceedings had
not yet commenced, but the place was
already crowded when Charity reached the
corner of this little square. She was later
than she intended. Above the heads of the
people she could distinguish Mrs. Mortimer
and Theodosia, sitting in state amidst the
élite of Babblemouth society. For her,
also, was reserved a seat upon the platform,
but how to get to it was more than she
could tell. For the crowd, although certainly good-natured, was in high spirits and
jocular with a coarseness from which she
shrank.

Close beside her a group of electors
loudly discussed the merits of Mr. Poltimore-Briggs. Charity had so long regarded

him with awe, that it startled her to hear
that great name thrown to the four winds
upon the breath of disparagement.

"Poltimore-Briggs! Who's Poltimore-
Briggs?" cried an elderly sharp-featured
little man, in a shrill voice, looking around
defiantly. "A fine fellow to put up for
Parliament indeed. Put up for sale, you'd
buy him dear at his own valuation. Why, I
remember when he was nobody. I was in
his father's office once — but that's out o'
memory. We can't call that to mind now.
He wasn't so big then. I say, that's his
house — that's his horses, walking up and
down for show there in front, — that's his
yacht out there covered with flags. Where
did he get it? That's what I want to know.
Why, out o' Lord Babblemouth's estate.
Eh? something clinging to the hand everything that's done. I tell 'ee what 't is, he
couldn't ha' got it if he hadn't robbed
somebody."

There was a general guffaw, for the little
man winked at every other word and talked
like an oracle.

Charity stood perplexed, wondering if it were possible to go on.

"Oh, come, come!" drawled a country-man, with a face round and red as a Dutch cheese; "we do know where the man picked up his money. His uncle Briggs died an' lef' it to un. I knew his uncle Briggs well, afore he died. Had a shop 'pon Finsbury Pavement, an' died sudden. Zold me hams for years. Hunderds o' hams. Capical hams, all sweet pickle. Ah! zixpence a poun' them times an' did well. Ha! Ha!" He laughed in happy recollection of those hams; and then added with deep earnestness, "But you can't do nothen out o' pig-butcheren nowadays."

"His uncle Briggs?" returned the other, fiercely, "under thirty thousand pounds, for I saw the will in the *Illustrated*. And Poltimore bought land wi' it, an' farmed it foolish ever since. And the land gone down half since then. And who knows who 's got the deeds, eh? Aha! oftentimes a man hasn't got all that goes in his name. No; what he got from his uncle Briggs couldn't do it. He stole it. That's what he did. He stole it."

"I stigmatise that as a lie. A paltry lie, imported for base party purposes. And any one who brings that tale here will very soon find himself in the wrong box. He'll soon learn the taste of Babble-mouth harbour."

Thus spoke the Babblemouth draper and undertaker, a tradesman of the first magnitude, whose fine feeling and tact in seasons of bereavement had earned him the respect of all. Many deceased members of the Poltimore family had he buried, only to gain thereby a deeper interest in the living. In virtuous indignation he strode two steps towards the little man, and looked fierce enough to kill him first and bury him afterwards. The little man fell back and butted against Charity. The undertaker bowed with reverence and apologised.

At this moment, by good fortune, the air was rent with cheers.

"Mr. Poltimore-Briggs — that is Mr. Poltimore-Briggs!"

Every eye turned towards the platform.
The landau traversed the fifty yards between
Mr. Poltimore-Briggs's house and the
wooden island in the sea of heads, and
safely deposited its precious freight. The
applause increased as Mr. Poltimore-
Briggs, followed by the orator, ascended the
steps. Yet there was opposition too, —
hooting and hissing, which lasted longer
than the cheers. The little man plucked
up and cried, —

" Booh ! "

To attempt to cross the square was useless, and Charity turned to go back. She
did not care about politics. Hooting and
cheers alike disturbed her, and her only
desire was to get away. Around by-streets,
now all deserted, she could reach Babblemouth House, and there await the return of
the politicians and the fireworks. Speeches
were nothing but weariness to her.

Amongst the old houses was one much
smaller than the rest, with a bay window
almost as big as itself. As Charity passed,
the front door quickly opened. Some one

spoke to her, and looking round she saw Alfred Prentice.

"Are you going home, Miss Chance? Will you come into my room? There is an excellent view of the people." His manner was distantly respectful, then suddenly dropped into tenderness. "Yes. Come, please, and talk to me just this once."

So this last meeting to which her mind was made up, had befallen by accident after all. Ought she to accept this invitation, so contrary to the code of Babblemouth? Yet why not? He too recognised the inevitable when pleading for just this once. It was only natural to wish to watch the crowd from some place of safety, and better far than going into the wood by design. Her thanks were scarcely audible. At once she passed through the open door, and followed him up the stairs.

The room shocked her sensibilities — it was so small and mean. The corners were not square. The ceiling was so low that a taller tenant might have touched it with his hand. It had not the dignity of a garret, for the bay-window was pretentious and the paltry furniture and tawdry German prints upon the wall marked it the lodging-keeper's own. Theodosia was right: he must be miserably poor. But how contemptible to tattle of it! And he too proud to accept their patronising hospitality. She loved him for that. She could have been proud herself.

She stood in the window, which came almost to the floor. The backs of the populace were towards her, but she was in full view of the platform. A stranger was now speaking. He majestically pointed to Mr. Poltimore-Briggs, and all the ladies clapped their hands.

"A strange ambition!" sighed Alfred Prentice, with the condescension of a lesser God looking down upon mortals, as he handed her a chair.

The little man had shouted an interruption, and was being hustled in the street below.

"They make it all personal. They mis-

represent so unjustly, when they only dis-
agree," cried the girl, impatiently.   She
recollected and resented the absurd attack
upon the integrity of Poltimore-Briggs.   To
know a person was, with her, to believe in
him; and dislike could not shake that
confidence.

Alfred Prentice looked at her intently.
She was excited, and her face glowed with
animation at the mere thought of injustice.

"I have missed you so much during these
last miserable days," he said slowly.   "I
have neither read nor worked.   I could not
concentrate my mind upon anything because
of a haunting fear that you despised me."

"Despised you!   That was impossible.
How could you think so?" she cried, almost
with resentment, for this pained her.

"You did not come into the wood.   The
interviews that were so precious, so rich in
profit to me, were at an end.   I had driven
you from your retreat; perhaps deprived you
of your greatest solace.   And that reflection was more bitter to me than my own
despair."

He nervously thrust his fingers through his long black hair. He was so emotional that he quivered with excitement at the sound of his own voice. Nothing could be more despairing than his utterance of the word "despair."

The loud aggression of the orator from a distance, driving home his points with the persuasiveness of a sledge-hammer, came through the open window, mingled with the laughter of the crowd. Every word was clear, but she did not hear what he was saying. She instinctively pushed back her chair. The people in the street were so close, they would witness her agitation and read her heart.

"I could see no good in coming after what you said. It could never be unsaid, or — or — forgotten," she told him sadly.

"No good!" he echoed. "When you were an inspiration to me. When every word was like the breath of spring, and the freshness of your belief in life gave me new hope, new faith, so that you became a necessity. No good!"

"I meant that — that nothing but unhappiness could result from our meeting each other. I felt it was not — not honourable. Yet I should have come once more if I had not seen you to-day."

Her voice sank. It sounded pitiful, this confession of weakness wrung from her in a moment of passion. It was a lament over a broken ideal.

He strode two steps across the little room, and threw himself upon his knees beside her chair. His arms were around her; his face was close to hers.

"Yes," he whispered fiercely. "You would have come because you love me. I know you love me; you cannot deny it, if you would. I can see it — I can hear it in your voice, and feel it in your presence here. But say it. Tell me the truth."

She could make no answer. Her tongue dared neither utter the secret of her heart, nor hide it in a lie. She made an effort to be free, but he held her fast.

"Say it," he insisted, and she could feel his breath upon her cheek. "A love unspoken is a song unsung — a jewel hidden from the light — a gift of heaven rejected. Tell me you love me."

His words were impetuous and irresistible. In a voice so low it scarcely seemed her own, she murmured, —

"I love you."

For a moment she abandoned herself to drift upon the full flood of acquiescence. She was carried, she knew not where, — far from the squalid little room to an island of enchantment and forgetfulness. The outbursts of the people in the street sounded far away, like the beating of summer breakers against distant rocks. One moment of joy and exultation, and she awoke with his kisses burning on her lips.

She tore herself away from him, and again stood up in the window. She was in a tumult of resentment, and crimson with shame.

"I am going now," she cried angrily, "I shall go straight home. I care nothing about the meeting. It is horrible to me, and I wish I had not come. Look! Look!

What are they doing there? They are
fighting. Where are they going to carry
the man?"

She pointed towards the quay-side.

The stranger whose contemptible party
spirit had been displayed in those absurd
comments upon the financial condition of
Mr. Poltimore-Briggs, by impertinent in-
terruptions brought upon himself the indignation of surrounding electors. "Duck
him! Duck him!" yelled the crowd. He
was seized on, and civil war raged around
his luckless body.

The girl looked on with horror, but Alfred
Prentice took little heed. To him it was
only an argument to defeat her intention.
"You must n't go yet," he said eagerly.
"It is not safe."

"I cannot stay. I ought not to have
come. But I wanted — I don't know what
it was — I wanted to say something — but
not that. I wanted to thank you — to show
that — "

Her anger had melted away, and in the
misery of hopelessness she burst into tears.

"Charity," he begged quite tenderly, "you have said you love me. Come away with me. To-night it is too late. We should get no carriage with all this foolery going on. But to-morrow — or next day."

She stared at him with her great astonished eyes.

"Do you mean run away?"

The frank wonder of the question made him hesitate.

"I mean take our destinies in our own hands, and live out our lives unfettered by other people."

"Whatever I do shall be avowed and open," she replied proudly. "Good-bye."

"It would be useless to tell. I am poor. They would not let you —"

"That would be nothing to me. Good-bye."

He did not take her proffered hand, and she turned hastily and went out of the door. He called after her by name. "Charity. One moment, Charity." But without a word she passed down the stairs and into the street. Fearlessly she pushed her way amongst the excited people on the outskirts of the crowd; but when she came upon the quiet road, she ran. Her great longing was to reach unheeded the solitude of her own room, and think.

But Miss Graham's quick ear heard her crossing the hall.

"What, Charity, back so soon! Come here, child."

"I was late, and the place was full. There was shouting and fighting. It was horrid, and I hated it."

"Of course you did," purred the little lady. "Why, you looked frightened into a fever. Graham ought to have known."

CHAPTER XII.

DISCLOSURES.

WHAT was she to do? Days passed; and this question, always present in Charity's mind, remained unanswered. She became silent and distraught. The affection of Miss Graham, expressed in a thousand delicate touches, to her difficulty heaped remorse. The girl could not steel her heart to hurt that tender friend. Thus life became a constant lie, and unbearable.

Amongst the summer hospitalities at Babblecombe House was one in which the little lady took peculiar delight. Once a year long deal tables were ranged upon the lawn, an urn of huge dimensions was hired from the town, and the workhouse girls were regaled with unlimited tea and buns.

It was early in the afternoon, and Miss Graham had been wheeled out of doors to await the arrival of her little guests. She loved to watch them coming along the road. To look at these hapless children quickened her sentiment and touched her heart.

"They are coming, Charity," she cried with enthusiasm. "Poor little things! How pretty they look in their blue cotton frocks."

The girl watched the procession marching two and two along the road. She was un-happy, and the sight to her seemed infinitely sad.

"I resent the blue frocks," she said warmly. "Why should they be marked for workhouse brats?"

The phrase sounded unkind. "Don't, dear, don't!" expostulated the little cripple, with a pained look. But as the children filed into the garden, her face beamed again, and she added: "How clean and well they look! Set them to play at once, Charity. The Mortimers will be here in a moment."

Scarcely were the words uttered when the expected visitors came hurrying into the garden.

"So sorry to be late," gushed Mrs. Mortimer, rushing up to the chair, and kissing Miss Graham upon both cheeks. "How are you, dear Miss Graham? It is so sweet of you. I have brought all the dear girls, you see, — to make themselves useful. Come, girls, come."

Her eye glanced from Theodosia to Amelia and Amy, and thence to the other six. The dear girls solemnly approached in single file, saluted Miss Graham according to priority of birth, and dispersed. Then Theodosia and her mother encamped upon stools, one on each side of the Bath-chair.

The sun shone gloriously. Swallows darted to and fro. The plaintive note of the greenfinch, like a sweet wail of recollected sorrow, came from the wood.

The workhouse children were ranged in two rows, playing one of those singing games, — the heritage for ever of the humble who have no toys.

" *We've a-come to see Jinny Jones, Jinny Jones, Jinny Jones,*
We've a-come to see Jinny Jones. How is she now?"

Backwards and forwards they tripped to
the rhythm of the song. The little cripple's face glowed with pleasure as she
nodded her head to the time. In heart she
was as young as they, and enjoyed the game
as much, — always at second hand. Their
little twinkling skirts awakened a joy more
tender than the early daffodils, or the bluebells in the wood. Something came over her.
She scarcely knew whether to laugh or cry.

"Jinny Jones is a-dying, a-dying, a-dying,
Jinny Jones is a-dying. You can't see her now."

Every one else being happy and busily
engaged, Mrs. Mortimer found the moment
propitious to push forward her sharp face
with the hook-nose she loved to put into
everything.

"I wanted to say something to you, dear
Miss Graham," she whispered mysteriously,
"if you won't be vexed with me. I speak
from a sense of duty and from the best and
kindest motives, and because I feel you
ought to know."

" What shall we dress her in, dress her in, dress her in ?
What shall we dress her in ——— dress her in now ?"

Miss Graham turned from the children with a sigh of regret. When Mrs. Mortimer spoke under moral compulsion, she always said something unpleasant.

"What is it?" she asked simply.

"It is about Miss Chance, — Charity, I mean. Dear Miss Graham, you know what the Babblemouth people are, and how they tattle." Mrs. Mortimer shook her head censoriously. "I would n't say a word myself for the world — only it is such a pity when a girl is talked about — "

"Talked about?" interposed Miss Graham, sharply. "Oh, yes. I have no doubt of it. Foolish idle tongues cannot be stopped. So much the worse for them."

"Ah! How true that is!" sighed Mrs. Mortimer. "And you know I have always felt the deepest regard for — for Charity. She is so spontaneous, so impulsive, one cannot help being in love with her. You see, we who know her understand and appreciate these good qualities. You and I, dear Miss Graham, see her true worth. And of course things are always exaggerated. Perhaps I may be wrong in detail, but I will find out —"

"There is nothing to find out in Charity," cried Miss Graham, warmly. "Her faults are all on the surface. She is so transparent that any one may see to the bottom of her soul."

"Yes. And how beautiful that always is — that real ingenuousness. It endears her, and makes one feel all the more that — that one must speak. But this Mr. Prentice with whom she has become so friendly — the poet, you know — Theodosia, you had better go and assist your sisters."

"Friendly with Mr. Prentice!" The little lady fired up, and her eyes flashed with indignation. "Friendly with Mr. Prentice! Why, she scarcely knows the fellow. She met him once at Graham's; and saw him afterwards in the wood, so she told me. That is all. Do you think she could speak to a real live genius with long hair, and not come home and talk of it?" In impatience with such nonsense, Miss Graham laughed outright, and abruptly turned her head to watch the children, still singing, —

" Black is for mourning, mourning, mourning,
Black is for mourning. That will do."

"Then I think, dear Miss Graham, you ought to be told the truth." Mrs. Mortimer pinched her thin lips in determination not to shrink from an unpleasant duty. "It would be no true kindness either to yourself or Charity to allow you to remain in ignorance. Besides, a word from you will do so much. It must, if there is any gratitude in this world."

She paused, shook her head in doubt, glanced at Charity towering so tall and graceful above the little cotton-clad paupers, and sinking her voice poured forth an unceasing stream of whispered gossip. On and on it gurgled, like rain out of a gargoyle on a wet day. How Charity had met Mr. Prentice by appointment at the rock on the hill-top, not once nor twice, but every day for a fortnight; and Mr. Prentice was there the first thing in the morning to the

11

last thing at night, so that Charity might run out when she could; for John Sprake had seen them, and John told William the coachman, who told Selina, *of course*, who, when she was dusting the dining-room the other morning, began to mention it — "not that I ever allow a servant of mine to utter one word about anybody, or listen to anything that is said; for I either check them at once, or give them a severe scolding afterwards; but when I found Charity going to his lodgings, and in fact with my own eyes saw her there on the evening of Mr. Poltimore-Briggs's meeting, I felt it my duty, for the sake of the girl herself, to let you know what is going on. I should have walked over on purpose if we had not been coming this afternoon, no matter at what inconvenience. Nothing should have prevented me."

Mrs. Mortimer, who had been drilling holes in the turf with the top of her parasol, suddenly looked up and cut short her harangue.

Miss Graham, sitting more than ever

erect, was white with anger and wounded pride. But the little lady did not lose her self-control. "You are very good indeed," she said, so calmly that the compliment sounded sincere, but so coldly that Mrs. Mortimer felt quite uncomfortable. "If Charity has talked to him unknown to me, no doubt the conversation was too unimportant to repeat."

Mrs. Mortimer fidgeted upon her campstool. Something within warned her to desist, but the temptation to tell was altogether too much for her. Moreover a relentless conscience commanded complete disclosure of the worst, — how Theodosia had overheard, — not that she listened, dear child, for none had a keener sense of honour than Theodosia, — had overheard the most terrible conversation that night when she was picking foxgloves for the decorations. So that at first the poor child, believing it must be Graham himself, from feelings of delicacy crept further into the wood, to let them pass by undisturbed. But when she saw who it was, she was astounded.

"Nobody knows what that poor thing suffered," sighed Mrs. Mortimer, from the depths of a mother's heart. "For two whole days and nights she never once closed her eyes, nor ate enough to keep a sparrow. She is so peculiarly sensitive to considerations of right and wrong, she dared not breathe a word for fear of being mean. She could not say her prayers with such a load upon her mind. She could not sleep. At last she sent for me — in such a burning fever that I thought of calling in Bibberley — and told me all. I gave her two globules of aconite at once, and exhausted nature slept like a child."

"I do not believe a word of it," cried Miss Graham, fiercely. "I have never known Charity do a wicked thing — or repeat an unkind one — or repeat an unkind one."

As she nodded to emphasise the repetition, Mrs. Mortimer winced and drew up her head.

"We know how you dote on Miss Chance, dear Miss Graham. It is only natural that you should. But others can be at least truthful. Let me call Theodosia?"

"I want no corroboration. Nothing would make me believe a word of it. Duplicity and deceit are contrary to Charity's nature. And you have always slighted and looked down upon her. Every one of you from the first. You are all envious of her."

Mrs. Mortimer clutched her parasol, for after all she was the rector's wife. "Envious — envious of Charity Chance!"

"Yes. Envious. Because she has more mind, and a finer temper, and a truer soul. Hundreds of times I have seen and resented it in my heart. I could never resent it openly, here in my own place. But now she is to marry Graham she is nearer to me. Not dearer, but closer. And everything affecting her touches me — touches me to the quick."

Whilst speaking, the little cripple unconsciously pressed her hand upon her bosom, and a red spot burned upon her pale cheek.

Mrs. Mortimer arose from her camp-stool

with a dignity so stupendous that nothing human could keep it up.

"As long as I live," she bounced out, "I will never try to do a good action again." The assertion sounded a little sweeping, and she stammered between hysterical sobs: "I mean — I mean — I meant merely to give a hint for the sake of the girl. I thought you ought to know. Envious of Charity Chance! Theodosia, you must walk home with me, dear. I am feeling a little upset. The other girls may stay if they have tempers fine enough and souls true enough to be of any service."

Without a protest from her indignant hostess, in consort with Theodosia she sailed past Charity, the workhouse children, and the wondering eight, and disappeared through the iron gates.

The singing had ceased. There was a lull in the games.

"Go on playing, children," urged Miss Graham, with a smile. She was so exasperated that she appeared calm. But the happiness of her little guests no longer gave delight. She was disturbed, humiliated, and the excitement had brought on her hidden pain. She had taken part in a vulgar altercation, — a scene. She detested Mrs. Mortimer for having moved her to anger. And yet, was this prejudice against Charity to last to the end of time? What could the child have done to raise such a report? Spoken to the fellow in the street, perhaps, and set these Babblemouth *canaille* barking. Met him by accident in the wood, and aroused the suspicions of Theodosia, indeed, who would have given her eyes to marry Graham. Yet a girl could not be too careful. She would say a word to Charity, tenderly, without wounding her sensibilities by telling how much Mrs. Mortimer had said. She sighed from the depths of her soul. Why was not everybody kindly and true and sweet? She shivered with mortification, there in the warm sun. She neither heard the tinkle of the tea-cups nor gloried in the demolition of the buns. And when the workhouse children at departure filed past to courtesy before her chair, she received each salutation as a matter of course, and was glad to get them gone. The Mortimer girls went also. She did not ask them to stay.

"Take me indoors, Charity. I will not wait for Sprake."

Charity wheeled the chair across the lawn to the French window, and together they slowly mounted the three steps. But safely upon the sofa Miss Graham still held the girl's arm.

"Sit down. I want you, child," she commanded in her abrupt way.

With a sinking heart Charity obeyed. Yet again a talk about her marriage, she thought.

In her refined tenderness the little lady hesitated, scarcely knowing how to begin. Then in a low voice she said, —

"Charity, as you go through life, dear, you will find thousands of things, indifferent in themselves, which nevertheless assume importance in their consequences. Since we have to live in the world, we must do as the world does. Not in its follies and frivolities, I do not mean that, but

in the observance of its little conventional-
ities. It does n't do to do everything that
has no harm in it. It is wiser to conform.
There is an art of living to be learned —
quite a fine art in its way. Now this Mr.
Prentice, whom they tell me you have —
How you tremble, child! I know there is
no harm of course — they say you have
met — "

"I love him. I love him with all my
heart."

The cry, sudden and passionate, was
both self-accusation and excuse. The gentle confidence and affection expressed in
every word Miss Graham had uttered, sank
into the girl's soul. The warm pressure of
those nervous fingers, still resting on her
arm like a caress, broke her spirit. She
burst into a flood of weeping. Better never
to have been born than to break the heart
that had taken and cherished her. Better
to be dead and in her grave. Then with
the caprice of passion she dashed away her
tears, shook off the restraining hand, and
stood up fearless and defiant.

"Yes. I love him," she cried again.

"Charity, you are beside yourself. You let your imagination run away with you. Why, you've scarcely seen the fellow. You are immodest — shameless — "

As she threw these words like missiles at the girl, the little cripple rose, and, quivering with excitement, leaned forward upon her ebony stick.

"I wanted to do what was true, but there was no help for me," wailed Charity. "It seemed so easy when I said I would marry Graham. It was to make everybody happy. That was my only thought. But I did not know my own heart. How could I know?"

"Mere midsummer madness!" cried Miss Graham, striking her stick upon the floor. "A month ago you had never set eyes upon this — this rhymer. A day or so and he will be gone. Do you think he will ever bestow a thought upon you? Or upon anything when the moment of his shallow vanity has passed?"

This contempt for Prentice stung Charity into resentment. No longer pleading for pity, her spirit arose in revolt against such injustice.

"Whether he is a rhymer or a poet, he loves me. He said so — "

"And you stooped to listen. You, having promised to marry, admitted this stranger to such familiarity that he dared to tell you so. No wonder they come to warn me. What they say is true. I can see it is true. You walked with the man you were to marry, and with his words still in your ears, you crept down into the wood at dusk to meet this mountebank. I can believe anything now. And you went to his room. Did you go to his room?"

Miss Graham stopped, but the girl did not answer. For a moment they looked at each other. The habitual sweetness had melted out of the little cripple's eyes. Only the nervous shrewd intelligence was left. Lifted above all tenderness and pity, she looked down from a height of virtuous indignation. And a sense of wrong hardened the girl's pride to adamant.

"I am ashamed!"

With a deep sigh Miss Graham turned away. All her hopes were dashed to the ground. Her dignity was broken. No words could express for her a deeper degradation. She hobbled a few steps toward the door; and then, overcome by the bitterness of disappointment and a sense of the girl's ingratitude, she could control herself no longer.

"Yes. I am ashamed — ashamed that all these years could do no more than this. I took you from the first. I fed you — clothed you — taught you from my own lips. Everything that could soil your mind or cast a stain upon your soul I kept from you. Everything that was noble and sweet and good, I set before your eyes. I poured it into your ears. I could not bear to let you out of my sight. When you came back from the school, I watched you, — your every step, every movement. I trembled lest vulgarity might have breathed upon you. I listened to every word, alert for a false note. I said, I will shelter her, and provide against every ill in life, except the inevitable sorrows that nature heaps upon us. But I was a fool for my pains. An utter fool! It is in the blood. I might have known it when they told me so. But it was all so pitiful that I seized you eagerly. I would hear no word of counsel. There are poor enough, in God's name, who are well-born. I might have taken a lady. I might at least have taken a child of decent folk —"

The girl moaned.

"Who was I?" she gasped.

Miss Graham felt no compunction. Her words ran on like a winter torrent, pitiless and cruel.

"You were nobody!" she cried. "A nameless child, cast away and picked up upon the quay. A workhouse brat, as you just now called them yourself, christened a grotesque name, the fanciful invention of a workhouse master. The pathos of it touched me. I must needs take you, fool that I was —"

"And everybody knows?"

"Everybody has always known but you.

I kept it from you. You might have gone to your grave no wiser if — "

But the girl had already fled. Through the French window, across the lawn, and past the shrubbery into the wood. There, like a thing wounded to death, she crept out of sight between the larch-trees and threw herself upon the ground. She wept and sobbed in a passion of misery and shame. She could not think. She did not feel. Even at the height of her agony came a moment of intense calm, when she told herself that she did not feel. Something was wanting, some moral sense, some quality of heart. One vital spark of true emotion and she must have loved Graham. One natural touch of tenderness and to bring sorrow upon the woman who loved her would have been more terrible than death.

She hid her face upon the brown earth. She pressed her cheek upon the dry larch spines. She wished that she was dead.

She was nothing. A friendless waif thrown upon the world to be picked up by charity. All her life had been unreal, and this was the awakening. Why was she not left upon the quay to die? Why was she taken from the workhouse to live a dream of joy, and wake into a terror of calamity? She clenched her teeth, and cried that it was cruel. It was not pity at all. Miss Graham had made a plaything of her. It was like Eve in Eden, where she needs must eat and be driven out upon the earth.

She must go. The quicker the better! Away from this place, where every object recalled her shame; from these Babble-mouth people who looked down upon her with such scorn. But whither? In her whole life was only one thing real, — her love for Prentice. And he loved her. He was a poet, with a heart above littleness, a sense beyond what was mean, — and he loved her. He would take her at once as he had wished to do. Her heart rose in exultation. He was poor, and she loved poverty. He would be great, and she gloried in greatness.

A sudden doubt clouded the momentary gleam. When he knew her story, would he

change? Would he marry a workhouse
foundling without a friend in the whole
world?

She cast the thought from her mind.
How mean even for a moment to have harboured it! With his vehement, generous
love for reality, he would laugh away the
prejudices of the narrow-minded world.
Was it her fault that she was Charity
Chance? She cried in anger, she would
rather be as she was than as the people
who came whispering malice and lies about
her. She would go to him at once.

She got up and shook the dead brown
spines from her white frock. She would
not cross the garden to the high-road.
Above the wood was a by-path leading into
Babblemouth, and she climbed up the hillside and stood a moment breathless upon
the steep. Evening was creeping on.
The harbour lamp glimmered dimly through
the fading light. So much the better. She
would reach the town unseen. Yet what
did it matter now? Babblemouth had
talked for years. A group of seafaring

men and loafers were talking now upon the
quay, as they had stood and talked the day
that she was found. She hated the little
hole, and all its people. Her only longing
was to go, and see the place no more.

The way winded through a deep hollow
where between banks abrupt and ragged she
was quite shut in. The solitude and wild-
ness were in keeping with her lot. Her
mind was made up. If he would take her,
she was ready. In her excitement she strode
on with impulsive haste.

Upon the road she met no one, but she
saw the people turn to look at her as she
hurried down the street. They knew her
for the foundling and charity-girl well
enough. Upon the quay the loafers had
stopped their gossip to gaze at a ·carriage
from "The George," drawn up before Mrs.
Dibbin's little bow-windowed house.

Her heart beat fast. This fell so aptly
with what he had said that it took away her
breath. She stopped, and for a moment
clutched the iron railings with one hand.
Then she went on again.

The door of the house was wide open, and before she had time to knock, Alfred Prentice came running down the stairs. Upon his arm was an overcoat, and in his hand a small travelling-bag, which he put down in the passage, to look at his watch. In great haste he almost pushed past Charity without recognition.

"Mr. Prentice," she whispered.

He threw the bag and coat into the carriage and came back to her.

"This is most delightfully opportune," he said, speaking very rapidly. "I have been called away suddenly, and there is only just time to catch the night train. An important editor wants to see me — "

"Something has happened," she gasped; "and I came to tell you."

Again he looked at the time.

"Come upstairs."

He beckoned and led the way, like a man of business with just one moment to spare. She followed with faltering courage. His most trivial utterance had always sounded sympathetic and full of feeling, but now there was no tenderness in his tone. Even in her agitation she noticed that he was pale and excited. He glanced nervously down at the carriage in the street, as if every moment were precious to him.

"I came to tell you that everything is over." Her passion was too real, and she too frank to withhold or disguise anything. "When you spoke to me the other day, I was not free. But they taxed me with meeting you, and I avowed it. I said I loved you. Nothing else was possible after all you have said to me. It would have been as if I were ashamed of what I am most proud. Then she told me I was a pauper, — a nobody, without a name to call my own. It is not possible to live at Babblecombe any longer. And I came to — to ask you what I must do."

He paced across the room, and anxiously back to the window. He was preoccupied, and she saw that he had heard her words without realising the blow which had fallen upon her. "You must do nothing rash," he said with grave deliberation, and paused.

Nothing rash! The most unpoetic soul on earth might utter trite wisdom such as that.

He passed his fingers through his long black hair. Then he caught sight of the look of wonder and terrified inquiry in her great frank eyes, and was himself again.

"Charity, you know how much I love you," he said in a voice quivering with emotion. "But I should be the meanest man who ever lived if I allowed my poor passion to weigh against your true welfare. You must go back to Miss Graham. Self-restraint is the secret of all true living. Nothing can alter our love. And I will think — and write to you. Yes, that will be the best thing. I will write to you. But I must go. It is important I must be in London to-morrow."

He was tender, magnanimous, prudent, and attentive to business, all in so many phrases. And it was all real too — as images in a reflection are real. Then he hurriedly kissed her, and ran to catch his train.

The driver cracked his whip; the carriage-wheels rattled over the stones with which the quay was paved; and he was gone.

And was this all the help that love could offer in her time of need? In her dream he had taken her to his arms. "Come, we will marry at once," he said, and carried her away into a new and brilliant future beyond reach of the past. She stood there, as motionless as Niobe in the midst of her dead hopes. Hidden and unsuspected forces were shaking the garden of ideals. The green island of inexperience was crumbling under her feet. For the earth had opened, and Charity Chance was on the brink of an abyss.

At last she aroused herself to return home. She did not notice the faded little yellow-haired woman who asked her whether Mr. Prentice lived there, as she was passing out of the door.

CHAPTER XIII.

CHARITY GONE.

CHARITY was gone!

Broken-hearted and purposeless she had crept home through the darkness to her little room over the porch, and cried away the night. Her spirit was benumbed. But dawn came rising above the brim of the hill, daylight poured into the coombe, and meadows and lawn glistened cold with morning dew. Another day was come. She bestirred herself to think what she must do. She must write to Graham. She seated herself at the table before the window and wrote him a letter imploring his pardon. She was unworthy of his love, had disgraced herself and him, had never deserved his confidence, and he must forget her. She had learned her own story, she told him, and should leave Babblemouth at once. Poor Graham! His goodness and fidelity touched her as she thought of her own inconstancy. She felt a tenderness towards the playmate of her childhood as she penned this farewell.

But where was she to go? No matter where, so long as she could earn her living out of sight of all who knew her. She must take the first thing that offered, no matter what.

It was very early, and no one in the house had moved. In idleness she had often scanned the columns of advertisements in *The Guardian*, a paper held by Miss Graham in high estimation; and now she fetched the last issue from downstairs, and set herself to search in earnest. Of money she knew nothing. Her wants had ever been anticipated. Vulgar considerations of cash lay submerged and unsuspected in a sea of unlimited credit, for payment of accounts looks almost poetic upon cheques of finest lithography and delicate tint. She quickly turned over the pages, but her eye first alighted upon the "situations wanted."

"*Lady Crowborough warmly recommends her governess. Thorough English, fluent French, German (acquired abroad), Latin, Drawing, Music, Singing, Calisthenics. — Miss R., the Library, Oldhurst, Berks.*"

Who would recommend her? Or what could she say for herself? With a sigh she turned over the leaf, but found no comfort. Here every accomplishment under the sun was wanted,—"*Good temper, disciplinarian. Must be a lady. Care of clothes. Photo and particulars. Stratford Rectory, Hants.*"

She clenched her teeth in anger. What did they mean with their "*must be a lady*"? She could not answer that.

In the whole range was only one that did not exclude her in advance. Mrs. Cornelius Porter of Forest Hill required a nursery governess to take charge of five children. *Must be experienced in teaching. Music essential. £15 to £25 according to qualifications.*

This at least displayed openness to argument, perhaps to conviction.

In her quick impulsive way she seized her pen. It was the mere clutching at a straw in her last hopelessness, but she wrote. She shivered to see what she had written, it looked so fraudulent, — and added she would gladly accept the lower sum on account of her inexperience. Then she stole out in the cheerless morning, and dropped both letters into the red post-box in the garden wall. Having thus taken her fate into her hands, she became more composed. She threw herself upon the bed and slept.

Some hours elapsed, and with a start she awoke. The sun was shining full into the window, and a maid was tapping at the door. Miss Graham sent word she was not well, and did not wish to be disturbed. To be alone was a relief to Charity, and yet the message cut her to the quick. It was considerate, but it marked the fall. How much weariness before now she had read away! How much pain she had soothed by merely sitting by the bedside! And that was over. Her conscience groaned under a burden of ingratitude. It told her again and again how deeply the little cripple loved her. And she had lost the wish of her heart.

When at last Charity went downstairs, the house was as silent as a grave. Even the servants moved mysteriously, and cast inquisitive glances at her red eyes and pale face. They knew all about her, like the rest of the world. Yes, the sooner she was gone the better.

Thus the miserable day passed — until evening. Then came a quick step across the hall, and unannounced Graham rushed into the room. His face was burnt by the sun, he was white with the dust of the road, and in his hand was the letter she had written him.

"What is the meaning of it, Charity?" In his resentment he could not wait for a reply. "What have they been saying to you? Who has dared to comment upon you? But I know what they have said.

They have even hinted it to me; and some fool sent me an anonymous letter. Do they think I care what they say? Charity dear, if every tongue on earth were to tattle about you, I should only love you the more. I know their gossip about Prentice. Of course you have talked to Prentice. There are very few to interest you in this place. I'm not half good enough for you, Charity, I know that. But I'm not such a fool as to listen to anything *they* say. Why, you can't do anything wrong or mean. You have a mind that won't let you. Charity, I think you are the noblest —"

"Oh, stop! stop!" she cried, placing her fingers upon her ears. He had seated himself upon the sofa beside her, and now he laid his hand upon her shoulder. But she shrank away from his touch. She got up quickly and crossed the room. Her back towards him, she leaned against the mantelpiece, and, burying her face upon her arms, she sobbed and sobbed.

Just as Miss Graham's delicate confidence, so her lover's absolute trust overwhelmed her with shame. He followed and stood by her side.

"Charity," he stammered, in a voice so low that it was scarcely audible, "I — I don't know how you have learnt your — your story. You once asked me, and I told you I did not know. But I always knew all there was to know. I thought — I mean if you thought I did not know, and that could make any difference — Charity, marry me at once. I have always known and loved you for yourself. Marry me now — before I go back."

How manly and true he was! She had never glimpsed into the depth of his character, through the light-hearted carelessness of his life. But he did not understand how his words wounded and hurt her.

She raised her head, and looked him in the face with frightened eyes beseeching pity.

"I shall never marry you, Graham," she cried wildly, "nor any one. You will never see me again. I shall go away at once. I shall never come back. I shall

hide my face for ever.   And you must forgive and forget me."

Neither argument nor entreaty could
sustain her against this torrent of passionate shame.   He knew that both were
useless, and his love itself forbade him to
persist.

Then his disappointment turned to self-
reproach.

"I shall never forget you, and there is
nothing to forgive.   It is my own fault.
I made you promise me.   I cared about
nothing so long as you said yes.   I was vain
enough to think it would all come right —"

Her face betrayed the depth of her distress.   Conscious of the cruelty of his
words, he suddenly stopped.   Then in a
voice subdued and quiet he went on: " But
you will stay with Aunt Helen.   It shall
not be difficult for you, Charity.   I will go
away — abroad."

There came a tap upon the door.   Then
it opened.

Miss Graham had heard him come into
the house, and wished to see him at once.

"I will come back and speak to you, Charity," he whispered as he went away.

What would he say when he had learnt the truth? His generosity had bruised her so sorely that if he might only despise and cast her from his heart it must be a relief. She returned to the sofa, and sat down and waited. He was so long that the time seemed endless. She began to wish for him, that she might learn of Miss Graham. At last she heard his step upon the stairs. But on it went across the hall. The door closed behind him, and he was gone. She felt as desolate as the marooned mariner by crime cut off from humanity, and left to perish upon a friendless shore.

On the second day came a letter in answer to her application, accepting Miss Charity Chance's services at £15 a year, and requesting that she would come at once. Again the message had been sent that Miss Graham would not rise to-day and did not wish to be disturbed. The girl did not know what to do. Her mind was made up. She had taken her life into her own hands,

and to-morrow she would go. This determination, without delay, she placed beyond
recall. She found her train, and bade Jan
Sprake despatch a telegram from Babblemouth when he went to exercise his horses.
Then she wrote a line, telling Miss Graham
what she had done, and asking if she might
see her once more.

The day she spent packing her one big
black trunk. Never in her life had she
been away even on a visit, and this had
been given her only to hold the superfluity
of her wardrobe. The number of her possessions, now all at once laid open to the
light, astonished and perplexed her. She
did not know what to take. There were
trinkets too, bestowed upon every occasion,
—at Christmas, at the New Year, and on
the anniversary of the day they called her
birthday. And the old pearl necklet fastened with such pride around her throat
when she started for the ball at Babblemouth last winter. The tenderest sentiment lingered around these gifts. She
wept that the little cripple's love had met

such poor requital. But she took none of them. She instinctively determined what was really personal, and the rest she left. It was evening before she had finished packing, locked the trunk, and put the key in her pocket.

Late that night Miss Graham sent for her.

The room was almost dark. One candle, in a tall silver candlestick, stood upon a table in the corner farthest from the bed. The curtains had been drawn, and the pillow, with Miss Graham's head upon it, was quite hidden from view.

Charity stood by the foot of the bed and waited.

"So you are going, Charity." The voice was slow and clear. Hundreds of times the girl had marked a like formal preciseness when some person not in favour unconsciously affronted the dignity of the little cripple. "And I may never see you again. I know that you must go. You could not stay, and I could not bear to have you here. But I wish to say that I am sorry — sorry for the words uttered in the

moment of anger. Don't speak, — don't
dare to speak to me, child. This going
for a governess is an absurdity. You are
no more fit to be governess than I am.
They will turn you out in three weeks.
But you have done it, and so you must go.
However, remember this, wherever you
are, I charge myself with your future and
you need have no anxiety. Beside the
candle is an envelope. You will have to
start by half-past nine, but I will see to
that. And when you leave this — this
place, I will think of something for you, if
I ever can think. Take the envelope and
leave me. Don't speak a word. I cannot
talk any more. And go to bed at once and
rest."

The girl was used to obey, and she
stepped towards the table to do as she was
bid. But in this thought for her future was
no tenderness. Disappointment had dissi-
pated the love and the delight, and only the
sensitive pride and shrewdness remained.
She glanced at the letter addressed to
"*Miss Charity Chance.*" From early child-

hood many a gift had come like this. Sometimes it lay upon her pillow when she woke. Or she found it on the table when she went to bed. It was easily thus, for the little cripple would hear no thanks. Had it ever before been anything but "*For my little one,*" "*To my dear child,*" and of late always "*To dear Charity*"? Doubtless it contained money. Well, come what may, she would keep herself or die. She withdrew her hand, and left the letter there untouched. Then without a word she went away.

On the following morning at the appointed time, Jan Sprake brought round the carriage to drive her to the station.

The fat horses crawled slowly up the hill. Charity glanced back at the little mansion, the lawn, and the shrubberies. But all were blurred and out of shape with tears. She could not see the eager face peering after her between the blind and window-shutter. Nor hear the words, half-lament and half-appeal, which sobbed from the bosom of the little cripple, —

"Oh, Charity!   Charity!"

At last the carriage turned over the hill-top.

And Charity was gone.

Her departure was a nine days' wonder in Babblemouth, and many and circumstantial were the stories hatched in the glowing imagination of that place.   They sprang into sudden life, — brilliant, startling, erratic, like dragon-flies in a summer sun. Miss Chance had come into the town to meet Mr. Prentice, as she had done every day for a month.   He left hurriedly to catch the evening train.   She rose in the morning, early, posted a letter, and ran away before the household was up.   They met at Bath, and went on to London together.   A commercial gentleman staying at "The George," who knew every soul on earth by sight, had seen them walking up and down on Swindon platform.   This was a plain tale, and found favour with prosaic mortals who drank beer in the little bar-parlour of the hotel.

A fiction more romantic told how Graham Poltimore waylaid Charity and Prentice together in the wood, fell upon Prentice, threatened to thrash him within an inch of his life if he dared again show his nose in the place, and cast off Charity, who ran away in the night, leaving a letter imploring Miss Graham's forgiveness, but hoping never to return to Babblemouth. This version, as being creditable to Graham Poltimore, was adopted for party purposes by the supporters of Mr. Poltimore-Briggs, until denied upon the authority of Jan Sprake, who drove Charity to the station. It was then found to have been a pure invention of the most dastardly character, set about to ruin the Poltimore-Briggs family in the eyes of the electorate.

It was then known to a certainty that Miss Graham turned Charity away from the house, and refusing food and comfort had taken to her bed. Poor Miss Graham! Very sad at her time of life — and so afflicted too. Well! she had always spent her money in the town, every penny of it.

Ay, and just beginning to get about again.
Every sympathetic tradesman who bent to
customers across his counter under the burden of a large family repeated this story.
Yet scarcely had the report quickened into
healthy circulation, when the great carriage
with the fat horses went rolling down the
wondering street.   Upon a cushion higher
than usual sat the little cripple; and if her
cheek was pale, her head was more than ever
erect.

When Charity disappeared beyond the
horizon, a smarting pride aroused Miss
Graham's spirit.   Through the dull aching
of her loss came a sharp pang as she thought
of Mrs. Mortimer.   That the event had
justified the warning given by that excellent woman made no difference at all.
Unconsciously that proud little heart harboured the more resentment.   Since Irene's
death she had suffered no blow like this,
and she summoned all her fortitude to show
a brave face to the world.   Her sorrow was
deep, — so much the deeper must it be
buried.   She rang for her hot water, and

dressed at once. And she wrapped Charity's departure in a tissue so fine that it cannot be deemed a fib.

"Put Miss Charity's room tidy," she said to the maid who was helping her downstairs. "Then lock the door and bring me the key. She may be away some time, and nothing shall be touched until she comes back."

"We must take great care of Miss Charity's myrtle, John, this winter," she told Jan Sprake when next he wheeled her chair round the garden. "I don't know what she will say if anything happens to it whilst she is away."

Such things repeated mystified the world. Outwardly she triumphed over herself, but in secret her courage failed. She knew that Charity would never come back. She was angry and regretful by turns, because the girl had not taken the envelope. The evenings began to get chilly. There was no music in the house, and she had not the heart to read. She was nervous, and wrote to Poltimore-Briggs to hurry on the settlement.

Within a week Mrs. Mortimer's curiosity

got the better of her pique. There was absolutely no reliable information, for Graham told nothing, and she was not even certain that the engagement was broken off. After all, one must not cherish anger, and the mortification of pride is a Christian virtue. So she magnanimously marched over to Babblecombe at the head of her daughters, and was quite cordially received.

"I could not help coming, dear Miss Graham," she acknowledged with perfect truth, "when I heard you were alone. So I came early, to have a long afternoon. And the girls wanted to ask, if it would not be too much trouble, if the tennis net might be put up. They can mark out the court themselves quite easily."

It would be no trouble whatever, Miss Graham assured them. So the maid ran, the young man who worked in the garden helped, Jan Sprake muttered and perspired, and the thing was done.

"So Charity has gone away, they tell me," said Mrs. Mortimer, settling down to be sympathetic.

"Oh, yes," chirped Miss Graham, and she did not wince.

"But not for long, I suppose?" The sweetness of Mrs. Mortimer became quite insinuating.

"It is not quite decided how long she will stay."

"You must miss her very much?"

"Yes."

The plucky little woman could not hide it all. In spite of herself the sadness would betray itself in her voice.

"Has she gone a long distance?" continued Mrs. Mortimer, greatly encouraged.

Miss Graham thought a moment before replying. Then she looked Mrs. Mortimer quite frankly in the face.

"I am not quite sure whether — I mean, I have some little delicacy in talking about it — for the present, that is. It was her own private affair, and Charity decided for herself. There are occasions in life when one must decide for oneself. And this was quite sudden. She got a letter one day, and went the next. She followed the dictates of her conscience, and I dared not influence her in the matter. But I do not think I must talk about it — just for the present."

"I would not hear a word for the world, — not for the whole world," cried the agonised Mrs. Mortimer, dramatically, putting her fingers to her ears to deliver Miss Graham from temptation. "What can have happened?" she was thinking to herself. A brilliant thought illuminated her brain.

Four-and-twenty hours later the Prentice stories were laughed to scorn in Babblemouth, and it was freely asserted that Miss Chance had received a mysterious communication from her natural friends.

But now the disinterested character of Mrs. Mortimer's visit was to be revealed.

"However, it was not to ask questions that I came," she went on, hiding her disappointment in an artificial smile. "When I heard you were alone, I spoke to the Rector at once. I said — perhaps dear Miss Graham would like Theodosia to be with her for a while, to be company for her, and to read to her, and so on. And if you would, dear Miss Graham, I would do my best to spare her, even if it were all the winter. I am sure she would be only too glad to do anything for your comfort."

A scarcely perceptible shudder shook that sensitive little creature. She did not accept the loan of Theodosia, but her thanks were profuse. She was not strong enough at present to entertain a visitor. It would be too dull for the poor girl — perhaps, a little later — she excused herself.

The dear girls came in glowing like tulips. They were hot, and filled the room. They were breathless, and consumed all the air. Their superabundant health jarred upon Miss Graham's sensibilities. Yet they did nothing amiss, and said nothing whatever. She could not help comparing them with Charity. Charity was as strong as they, yet fifty Charities could not have been so obtrusive.

"Perhaps Miss Graham will allow you to come again," suggested their mother when they rose to depart.

They came again. In a little while they

came daily, and brought their friends. They went on playing, right into the winter, when the grass was wet and slippery, and they trampled down the Christmas roses searching for the balls. The lawn got bald in patches. "So bare as the back o' your han'," said Jan Sprake.

And the little cripple, with whom none before had ever dared to take a liberty, looked on in silence. She did not care about anything now Charity was gone.

CHAPTER XIV.

THE SETTLEMENT.

THUS the months passed until spring came, and again the meadows of the coombe were studded with daffodils. But there was no longer any glory in their gold, and Miss Graham scarcely turned her head to look at them. A fear as dark as winter clouded all her thoughts and chilled her heart. She dreaded to hear that Charity had married Prentice; for dearly still she loved the girl, and her dislike to this man — to whom she had never spoken — was instinctive and deeper than prejudice. It worried her, too, that Poltimore-Briggs, being engrossed in public business, found no time to attend to her request about the settlement. This neglect irritated her the more since he had almost a personal interest in the matter. A gentleman, she told herself in her proud way, under such circumstances, would not lose a moment. She began to suspect him of purposely putting it off. Mistrust settled like a dust in the mansion of her mind, and to know it there hurt her self-respect. She worried herself with thoughts of taking the matter into her own hands by altering her will, and procrastinated through fear of hurting the feelings of Poltimore-Briggs. And she had no one to share the burden of this anxiety, for Graham had gone away.

The dread haunted her that "something would happen" before her wishes were fulfilled. At last she wrote to Poltimore-Briggs, telling him to take no further trouble. She had changed her mind, she said, and determined to leave not only the money as arranged, but the Babblecombe estate to Charity. It would not be long to wait.

He replied in haste that the business was already put in hand, and urging her to do nothing until she had seen him. He would come to Babblecombe in a few days, he promised. But weeks passed, and her wishes were still neglected. The early summer came, and she had heard nothing further.

One afternoon in June she was sitting out of the sun in the old corner by the yew-hedge. The Mortimers were not there that day. It was quiet, and she was able to think. The time for the garden party drew close upon her, and she was wondering what she would do. Every year since she came to Babblecombe had this great function taken place without a break. But now she was weighing inclination against duty. She did not feel fit for it. She could not bear the fatigue. Yet responsibilities rest upon wealth and position, and she recognised her obligation to the neighbourhood.

Strangers would inquire about Charity —and what was she to tell them? And if she did not have it, the Babblemouth people would talk, and say she moped because the girl was gone. A dozen times she changed

her mind, and still came no nearer to a decision. Then her meditations were disturbed.
The gate fell to behind an approaching
visitor, and Poltimore-Briggs walked up
the path.

She was aware of something unusual in
his appearance. He had walked from
Babblemouth, and his boots were white
with the dust of the summer road. That
in itself was strange. For years she had
not known him go so far on foot. And his
face looked altered. It was thinner than
formerly, and quite pale and drawn from
anxiety and overwork. At once her doubts
were changed to sympathy. He had managed everything so well for years, and now,
when he was overwhelmed with cares, her
thoughts had been ungenerous and unjust.
She welcomed him warmly. For a moment
she held his hand quite affectionately, then
pointed abruptly to the seat by her side.

"I have been hoping to see you, Henry,
for a long time," she said. "And now I
cannot help feeling how kind it is of you
to come."

He sat down slowly, in obedience to her gesture. With one elbow upon his knee he leaned forward, and, resting his forehead upon his hand, looked down at the yellow gravel.

"I know, Helen. I have been remiss, I know," he stammered uneasily. "But I haven't been able to call my soul my own. Not for years, — I mean for months, — since I undertook this Parliamentary business. Otherwise your wishes would have received my first attention — as they always did, Helen — "

"Yes, yes. I don't know how I should have managed," she said warmly, and with real gratitude. Her quick eye observed him attentively. His white waistcoat, always so spotless, was soiled with the dust, and there was a black mark from the rubbing of the long gold chain. "He knows he will lose the election," she thought, "and that is a blow to his pride." At the sight of his dejection a dead kindness revived, — a tenderness of long ago, when a lover, spic and span, used to steal

to the old house in Bath, at the hour when
her father was from home. It seemed only
yesterday. She pitied him. Life is so
little, yet disappointment goes so deep.
All that she understood, as in mute
sympathy she laid her hand upon his
shoulder.

"And you must not altogether blame
me," he went on quickly, in self-defence.
"These lawyers are so dilatory. But I
have looked over the deed at last. It will
be ready to sign in a few days. I quite
agree that you could do no less. I have
made it that should she die without issue
the money will come back to Graham, or
his children if he have any."

"How wonderfully you think of everything!" she cried in admiration. And this
was the man whom she had suspected.

"But I came over to speak about something else. I — I want you to do me a
favour, Helen."

"Of course. Of course." In her contrition she was quite eager to grant him
his request unheard.

He moved restlessly in his chair. He was so nervous that his hand shook like a drunkard's, and he kept swallowing as if something choked his utterance. Then, reassured by the readiness of her consent, he found his tongue at last.

"Some years ago I made a very bad investment. A speculation, in fact, which proved disastrous. Anybody might have been deceived. And since then I have been — eh — hampered — at times sorely hampered for — eh — ready money. And we have lived extravagantly, I own that. Mrs. Poltimore-Briggs and myself have never — well, have never got on. Everything would have been different if poor Irene had lived."

He stopped and sighed. Deep in his heart, then, was still the recollection of Irene. No misfortune could have recommended him to the pity of the little cripple like this one touch of sentiment.

"And you want money, Henry?" she cried quite cheerfully.

A gleam of eager expectation flashed

across his face. He drew a long breath,
and sat upright as if in relief from a heavy
burden. He became more himself, and
regained something of the large manner she
had always disliked so much.

"The fact is, a man is pressing me at
a very inconvenient moment. There is
political animus without question. But
that makes it the more incumbent to meet
him without delay. I should prefer, if
possible, not to postpone payment a day.
Of course, in a week or so, when rents
come in, and so on, it would be easy enough.
But I will admit to you, Helen, candidly
admit to you, my self-esteem — my — my
pride will not permit me to ask a favour.
If you could lend me a couple of hundred
pounds, — say until the beginning of next
month, when I pay you your dividends, you
would do me a great service. I should be
really grateful."

His momentary elation had subsided, and
he leaned forward in anxiety for her reply.

Was that all, she thought, and felt quite
glad to be of use. Yet to a vain man it
must be hard indeed to ask.

"Of course, there is no difficulty about that. I should have had to get you to take care of it, so it is quite the same thing," she told him, laughing to make light of his needless distress.

"Could I have it before the bank closes, Helen?"

Leaning upon her ebony stick, she rose. "No. Don't move. I can go very well. Stay here in the cool and rest. I will go in and write you a cheque."

He watched her slowly pass along the path, until by the steps into the drawing-room she stopped to rest. Then she turned towards him and asked, "Are you sure that will be enough?"

He hesitated a moment.

"Yes, quite enough," he answered hoarsely.

The time was endless until her return, and he kept glancing at the open door. His dejection had vanished. He had taken heart at her readiness to assist him. His head was raised, alert and listening for the slightest sound; but in his uncontrollable impatience he bit his nails to the quick.

At last she came.

The serenity of human kindness smiled upon her face as she beckoned to him before cautiously descending the step. She had enclosed the cheque in an envelope. That looked so much less like lending money. She carelessly handed it to him between her long thin fingers.

"Come, I must not keep you."

Her tone was dictatorial, as it sometimes used to be with Charity. She did not give him time to speak, but, taking his arm, turned towards the entrance gates.

"I have handed over my hoard; so now, until you bring me more, I shall be penniless," she laughed gaily. Then her voice sank into a whisper, tender and confidential. "But make what use you like of it. What you have told me quite troubles me, Henry. It makes me feel that things have not been just. It is wrong, of course, but the very poor do not appeal to me like people who have been affluent and become pinched. That seems so painful — to be straitened and pinched. I could never have lived if I had been driven to worry about pennies. But there is nothing to save for now. Graham will have plenty. Charity you have seen to. There is nothing wanting — that money can supply. And my little superfluity, I suppose, may make all the difference to you?"

They were at the corner of the house, and she stopped, waiting for an answer to her inquiry.

But her kindness touched him. He looked quite dazed, and could not speak.

"Will not that make it right? At least, whilst I am here. And then Graham is goodness itself."

She spoke so cheerfully, making the best of it to comfort a sad heart, that he made an effort to cover his confusion.

"God bless you, Helen. God bless you," he stammered with emotion.

She held out her hand quickly to prevent his thanks.

"Good-bye."

"Good-bye."

He was so deadly white, and stared at her

so strangely that she was filled with alarm. He staggered as he turned towards the gate.

Between the stable-yard and the Babble-mouth road is a low stone wall, and above it a slanting laurel hedge. There, a short distance away, Jan Sprake was trimming back pretentious shoots which pressed before their fellows.

"You are not well. You ought not to walk in the sun. Let me have you driven," she urged anxiously.

He shook his head in refusal. "I — I did not wish my visit known," was all he said. Then he waved his hand to her and was gone.

Jan Sprake peered down at him inquisitively as he passed down the road.

Beside the laurel hedge he stopped, opened the envelope Miss Graham had given him, and drew out "a long leaf o' paper like." He was so close that Jan could have read the wording himself, if he "had but a-bin a bit of a scholard." His hand shook like an ague. The man cried like the rain.

"Poor Helen! Poor little Helen!"

Those were the words he muttered, Jan could take his Bible oath of it, any day of the week. Then of a sudden he tore the paper into shreds, and threw them fluttering upon the road-side. For many a summer day the tiny pink scraps lay there amongst the dusty grass in silent testimony to the truth of Jan Sprake's statement. And Poltimore-Briggs did not go straight home to Babblemouth. He turned off where a lane leads to the pathway over the cliff. Jan Sprake stood among the laurels and, wondering, watched him out of sight.

On the afternoon of the following day there rustled around Babblemouth a rumour so ridiculous that no one with any sense in his head could find patience to listen to it. Nevertheless, being constantly repeated, it grew and grew. It was said that bailiffs had been in the house of Mr. Poltimore-Briggs for a week past, and a sheriff's officer was aboard the yacht.

Certainly this had been kept marvellously

quiet, but things will leak out at last. Servants will talk. A leading tradesman of the town first got wind of it, and without delay strolled mysteriously down to the house to present his little account. Mr. Poltimore-Briggs was not in. The man would wait. Mr. Poltimore-Briggs was away from home.

The matter was of particular importance, and could Mrs. Poltimore-Briggs grant the favour of Mr. Poltimore Briggs's present address? But Mr. Poltimore-Briggs had been called unexpectedly to London, and his address was uncertain.

Before night the little town was all astir. It became known to all the world that Poltimore-Briggs, having laid hands on every penny he could get hold of, had absconded, it was believed, to Spain. And not an hour too soon. There was vague talk of money obtained by fraudulent representations, and it was no secret that a warrant had been issued for his apprehension. The place was in a ferment. Political opponents had always anticipated that something of the sort must happen one of these days. Supporters, who for the most part were also creditors, declared that he was the last man upon earth of whom any one would have thought it. There were bets at "The George" as to how soon he would be taken.

Only one person remained in ignorance of these proceedings. Little Miss Graham, happy in the belief that she had helped him over his difficulty, was the last to hear. The thing was altogether so unexpected and astounding that for the moment Mrs. Mortimer was mute.

CHAPTER XV.

AS NURSERY GOVERNESS.

A LONG room covered from floor to ceiling
with a yellow, varnished, washable paper,
except in one corner, where delinquent
finger-nails had picked bare patches before
Charity came. How the wall glistened
behind the solitary gas-jet jutting out
above the mantelpiece! The flame was
naked, the children having long ago smashed
the globe, which had not been replaced.
And it had to be kept low, being liable to
flare and run wild when turned up. But
everything in the place was bare, except
the spiritless little fire fast sinking to dust
and ashes behind the bars of an iron fire-
guard. Maria, the housemaid, had forgotten to bring up more coal.

It was late at night. The children were long ago in bed and asleep, and Charity had been sitting up at work. Her supper, sent upstairs on a tray, remained untouched upon the little ink-stained table by her side, just where Maria had banged it down some hours before, when she flounced in and flounced out, slamming the door behind her as a protest against waiting upon anybody who got no more wages than herself. That was the knell of parting day. Nobody ever came near Charity after that.

Dispirited and exhausted, she leaned back in her chair. The light glared upon her face. From the opposite wall a map of the world in hemispheres stared down at her, shining and binocular. She lifted a pile of papers from her lap and placed them on the table.

"How poor it all is!" she cried, and burst into tears.

The ugliness of the place was as remote from her mind as the antipodes. It was the last moan of a struggling swimmer who, overcome with fatigue, consents to sink.

The whole course of her miserable exist-
ence since she entered the service of Mrs.
Cornelius Porter passed through her mind.

She had now been a nursery governess for
months, and was accustomed to her duties.
At first, to her inexperience, the thing was
hopeless. But from the day of her arrival
she grappled with her difficulties with the
grim fierceness of despair. It seemed to
her that if she failed to fill that place there
was no other for her in the world. And a
quite extravagant success rewarded her
efforts. Before the second week was out
Mrs. Cornelius Porter, a middle-aged
matron, well nourished, and of the finest
Britannia-metal, intimated to Miss Chance
that with a little closer attention to the
darning she was likely to give every
satisfaction.

They were a prosaic race, these Porters,
and their days were all alike.

They breakfasted at half-past seven in
order that Mr. Porter might catch a train.
Upon this point Mrs. Porter waxed senti-
mental to the verge of poetry. If the chil-

dren were not there, they would never see
their father, and that was so sad. Daily
at this hour, expectant and somewhat overawed, they were ranged around the table.
At a quarter before eight Mr. Porter appeared, late, hurried, and inclined to be
irritable. He glanced hastily at the great
gilt timepiece upon the mantel-shelf.

"Eight minutes and a half," he muttered
morosely, "if the clock is right."

"The clock is always right," retorted his
wife; and it was a dogma for which she
would have died.

"Always?"

"Always!"

He swallowed his boiling coffee, bolted
his roll, flashed across the little domestic
heaven like a meteor, and was gone.

A nervous, sallow little man, with a long
black beard, who returned at eight in the
evening. That was all Charity knew, for
only once had she been privileged to speak
to him.

"You will take supper with us to-night,
Miss Chance," exclaimed Mrs. Porter, on

the afternoon of Charity's arrival, "and see Mr. Porter. Afterwards, perhaps you will play us something. We are both anxious about the children's music. You noticed *music essential*, I have no doubt. Oh! and I hope you don't mind making your own bed. Any other little thing I will mention as it arises."

The girl was nervous and uneasy, and the ordeal of playing haunted her through a silent, melancholy meal. It was to be a test of her ability, and, feeling it to be such, when the time came she played with care. The familiar sonata was like company to her in the strange place, but she rose from the piano dissatisfied and in doubt.

"Now, do you *really* like classical music, Miss Chance?" asked Mr. Porter, in that confidential tone which invites and deserves a candid reply.

Charity pledged her word to it.

"Well, I don't know," he reflected. "I like something a little gay. What's the use of music, except to take you out of yourself after a day's work, and 'liven you up a

bit? Now, classical music always makes
me feel unwell."

"We have a little music on Sunday after-
noons, Miss Chance," put in Mrs. Porter,
in fulfilment of her promise to mention
little things that might arise. "Mr. Porter
is at home, and it is nice for the children
to come down. Now you would like to go
upstairs."

Charity did not see much of Mr. Porter
on those occasions. She played hymn
tunes by the hour, whilst the children
sang. But the head of the house, hidden
in a silk handkerchief, reposed on a red
sofa-cushion and restfully slept.

Charity had never seen people like these.
Sometimes their destitution in the perception of everything that made life beautiful
to her was more pitiful than the sight of
poverty. The atmosphere of the house
oppressed her like a nightmare. The children overwhelmed her with a weight of care
under which she could scarcely breathe.
They broke everything. They hurt themselves and each other. They quarrelled and

cried. They were more mischievous than goblins without the mirth. And when she had struggled with all her might, the good-will of Mrs. Porter came like a last straw added to her load.

With the desire to be kind, that most respectable matron became inquisitive.

"And how many years did you live with Miss Graham?" "And where is your own home, Miss Chance?" were amongst the friendly inquiries with which poor Charity was plied.

For some time the discomforts of her new position had no power to wound her deeply. She hardened herself against everything with the great thought that Prentice had promised to write. As the days passed and nothing came, she became more wildly expectant. She studied the table of "inward mails," and listened for the postman's knock. Surely it would come now. Other letters delivered at Babblecombe were sent on, but the one so madly desired was not amongst them. She became a prey to all the fears and doubts that love can conjure

15

out of longing and disappointment. He
had changed towards her. Found out her
story and changed before she went to him.
How else should one so emotional, so sensitive to the slightest word, remain unmoved
by her deep humiliation? She might write
to him under cover to Messrs. Pickering
and Co., his publishers. She fetched his
book to find the address upon the title-page.
Then she grew proud again. He had
parted from her with no word of love or
help or kindness. He was angry with her
boldness in rushing to him so eagerly, and
disgust upon the instant changed so sensitive a man. Or perhaps prudence had made
him silent. He was poor — had not means
to marry; and in a calmer moment became
wise. With that thought again she loved
him tenderly. He would never change,
and her heart was his through all eternity.

At last the hope of hearing from him
waned. Then in the after-supper solitude
she fell to taking up the threads of her old
life. But the strands were all ravelled and
tangled. Nothing remained unbroken but

the slender story she had tried to weave in the leisure of her girlish happiness, and that lay at the bottom of the great black trunk, untouched by fate or fortune. She thought of it, and brought it to the light.

Now she read with other eyes, and saw with deeper insight. What she had written was but idle fancy-work, beside the gorgeous fabric woven in the loom of human life. It was a village tragedy, and the story held and fascinated her as at first. But when she wrote she had not understood. Passion and shame had come, — crushing self-abasement had fallen upon her since then. A hurricane had swept away the rose-clad walls that sheltered whilst they shut her in from the world. And she stood alone — nothing, unless she could be something of herself. A hope, familiar of old in the dappled sunlight of her hill-side bower, revived within her. She would make something of that story. In growing excitement she rose and paced the narrow little school-room. Her brain was in a ferment, her soul on fire. Yes. She, the nameless, base-born foundling, would win herself a name.

Not a moment must be lost. She drew a chair to the table and sat down before the sheets, all faultlessly copied in the days when time was plentiful and she had little to do.

The opening chapter was poor, indeed. But she would improve that. Her fingers burned to begin at once. She fetched the ink, and pen in hand set to work to read. All night through she went on, scoring, interlining, and blotting out until only here and there the girlish penmanship, like the pale face of a prisoner condemned to death, peered through the prison bars of her ruthless alterations.

She laid aside the pen and burst into tears to see what she had done. So this, like all the rest, was nothing. It would be far easier to begin afresh. With a heavy heart she put it all away until another night. But from that time forth, the expectation of these silent hours triumphed over the drudgery of the day, and she was never lonely and never without hope.

She worked with such eagerness that the story grew apace. It held her imagination with a force so vivid and irresistible that her real life passed like a dream, and this phantasy assumed the boldness of reality. It was interwoven with her deepest emotions. Not that she confided to the page the secrets of her heart, but the romance of it glowed with her passion for Prentice, and the tenderness was a recollection of her love for the little cripple, and to the misery her own pride and shame gave bitterness.

Last night with a thrill of joy she finished. To-night she had read it from beginning to end. Now she turned round to her dusty little fire, and in spite of herself the words sobbed up from the bottom of her heart,—

"How poor it all is!"

In her enthusiasm she had hoped so much. It was to redeem her from drudgery —to make her worthy of Prentice—to prove the little cripple's kindness not all in vain. She had resolved to send it to Prentice's publisher. But what avail to send it anywhere? No one would look at it. It was poorer than before, and with this hopeless difference,— that then she altered without hesitation, and now, for the life of her, she did not know what more to do.

Nothing more could be done, and she cast the papers from her in disgust. Suddenly the door opened; the portly figure of Mrs. Cornelius Porter, magnificent in a brocaded evening wrap, sailed into the room. "You are sitting up very late, Miss Chance," she said severely. "I saw the light in your window as we came in, and Maria tells me you always sit up half the night. It is quite impossible you should do your daily duty, unless you retire at a reasonable hour and take proper rest. I must request that by eleven, so long as you remain in this house, — not later than eleven, — your gas shall always be turned out."

There was an assumption of superiority in the tone which Charity had never before noticed. Vulgar the woman had always been, but good-natured enough, and even kind. Now she stood there large and arrogant. The very glance which she threw down upon the girl was an insult.

"I had something to do for myself, and no other time to do it," returned Charity, coldly. "But now it is finished."

The answer sounded rebellious, and did not please Mrs. Porter.

"I think I ought to tell you, Miss Chance," she went on, with the satisfaction which a small soul lodged in a comfortable body takes in the contemplation of its own virtue, "that I have heard a great deal about you to-day. A gentleman who visits Babble-mouth regularly on business has told us all. He says you were the talk of the town. He even saw you himself at Swindon Station."

"He is mistaken," interrupted the astonished girl; "I have never in my life been to Swindon."

"At Swindon Station," repeated Mrs. Porter, with louder firmness. "In what class of company I should be ashamed to say. You can read for yourself in yesterday's paper. Then no further comment of mine will be required. I need not add that you can scarcely expect to retain a home in a respectable family."

With this withering sarcasm Mrs. Cornelius Porter left Charity to her perplexity. There was more of Cornelius than Porter in the dignity of her bearing as she passed out of the schoolroom door.

"Swindon Station," the girl kept repeating. "What does she mean by Swindon Station?"

If an apparition had broken in upon her midnight vigil, she could not have been more bewildered. An awful suspicion crossed her mind that an evening's entertainment must have resulted in the incoherency of Mrs. Porter. The thought was so horrible that for the moment Charity forgot she was again a waif. Anything to get away from such people and such a place. In desperation she got up, packed the re-written story, poor as it was, and addressed it.

She left it ready upon the table. In the morning she rose earlier than usual, and ran out with it to the post. Her heart sank within her as the packet fell with a thud into the letter-box.

But Mrs. Porter's words, "You can read for yourself in yesterday's paper," kept ringing in her ears as she hurried back to the house. She would go into the dining-room and see what that meant. The fire was as yet unlighted. She was fortunate enough to rescue the newspaper from the scuttle of Maria, and she glanced at the headlines as she carried it upstairs.

The Prentice Case.

Breathless she stopped beside the landing-window to read. It was a suit brought against the poet by his wife.

"Married! Impossible! A lie begotten of envy to besmirch the reputation of a man of genius."

With this cry of passionate and indignant denial, she threw down the paper in angry refusal to learn evil of one she loved. It was like listening to a tale behind his back. Then that was why she had not heard. How could he write under the weight of this great trouble? How deeply this must cut his pride! Yet she must read to learn how much he suffered,— to hear his refutation and delight in his triumph.

She picked up the newspaper and carried it to her schoolroom. There was still time to spare before the day began, and she glanced down the long columns, and eagerly turned to read. But as she went on she grew sick at heart. The print became dim before her eyes. It was a tale of heartless desertion, and in spite of herself the woman's misery forced itself upon her sympathies.

"But they were unhappy, unsuited to each other," she cried, in contradiction to herself. "It was pitiable, but they were wise to part."

Then Prentice came into the witness-box, bantering with counsel. He treated the matter lightly, and was witty merely for effect. He, who had talked so sadly of human woe, as if the weight of all humanity oppressed his soul, went through the tragedy of his own making grinning like a

comedian. The words of Miss Graham
came back to her, — that underneath the
folly of genius was soul or passion or a
great heart. And this man had none of
these. Her illusion was dispelled. She
could not look at this and longer believe in
him.

And for him she had forfeited an affection which had enriched her life. Then his
love was all the world, but now, in the
moment of her disenchantment, how she
longed for the tenderness of her one friend,
— the friend who had given everything, —
the benefactress who, deceived and disap-
pointed, turned away her face in shame.
She wanted to make amends. If she might
only say, "You were right, but I knew no
better then," and feel just once, in understanding and sympathy, the pressure of
the little cripple's cheek against her hair,
she could take heart against the world's
vulgarity. There came to her an impulse
to go back, — just for one day, — to
give her gratitude expression and implore
forgiveness —

The shutting of a door at the other end of the passage broke in upon her thoughts. In a few weeks she would be homeless. It would look like beggary even to write to Babblemouth at this moment. And she was only Charity Chance, after all. She hastily laid aside the paper. She had loitered too long, and already the steps of Mrs. Cornelius Porter were creaking down the stairs.

It was now the early spring, and Charity once more found herself face to face with the problem of how to earn her bread. She was to leave in the summer. "That will be the most convenient, and give both parties time to look around," explained Mrs. Porter, thinking only of herself. "And anything that I can say as to your competency, Miss Chance, I shall be very pleased, I am sure." At once the girl began to scan and answer advertisements. But the time was too far off, and no one ever applied to Mrs. Porter.

Now that the manuscript was gone, her evenings were lonely, indeed. The little

group of phantoms vanished from her
hearth. Their story faded into the forgotten past. She had no hope that any one
would print it, but to write had been a
relief, and out of the ferment of her emotions a new fable began to take shape in her
imagination. Then, again, she forgot her
troubles in work.

Yet her mind was alert with expectation.
She looked for no great tidings; nevertheless, as days grew into weeks and no answer
came, she became conscious of the depth of
her disappointment. She began to fear.
The parcel might have gone wrong. Perhaps it was lost. Perhaps, unsolicited, it
should not have been sent, and therefore,
being useless, had not been returned. She
realised that it was nothing, and yet she
was consumed with anxiety.

One evening, having laid down the
supper-tray, Maria loitered.

"There's a letter, Miss Chance, came last
week. It was left in the kitchen. I meant
to bring it up, and then I forgot it. I hope
it isn't any difference, I'm sure."

Fully determined to demean herself no further, Maria withdrew in haste.

The publisher's device was upon the envelope. So there was to be a verdict, after all. Now that the time was come, although she had no hope, her agitation was so intense that her trembling fingers could not break the seal. Then, with sudden nervous energy, she tore it open.

The contents were very brief, but glancing over the letter her eye caught in snatches the whole pith of the matter.

"*Prepared to undertake the publication of the same . . . of course with an author's first work it is not possible to offer . . . royalty of* 10 *per cent, upon which we would pay a small sum — say £*20*— upon account.*"

A commonplace communication, sure enough, yet one which read with all the wealth and wonder of an Arabian romance. Twenty pounds! Now that she had earned it herself, it was a mine as inexhaustible as the Indies. Her imagination ran riot over the magnificence of the sum. And royalties run on for ever. The occasion

justified a revel, and she took it in elemen-
tary arithmetic. Twenty pounds! She had
rewritten the book in six weeks. She
would finish the new one by June. Twenty
and twenty make forty, and then her stipend.
She would walk out into the world worth
fifty pounds. Then she would take a room,
and write, and write.

But the latter portion of the letter was
still unread.

"*Should you accept these terms, please
reply without delay, as we should like to print
at once, to publish in our series during May.*"

And a week had elapsed! They might
refuse to stand to their offer now. At once
she wrote a letter of acceptance loaded with
apologies. They replied with a printed
contract. Then proofs showered down upon
her. Revises followed like the April rain.
At last came that early copy of the first
book, a joy like the gladness of a new
spring. She turned it over in her hand,
and a thrill of pride leapt within her bosom.
She, the nameless waif, was about to jus-
tify her being.

CHAPTER XVI.

THE END.

CHARITY had taken apartments — two rooms the size of cupboards — in a little street near the residence of the Porters, and here she worked in peace. Her only luxury was a daily paper, which she searched for a review. The purchase was an excitement, like drawing from a lucky-bag; but once or twice she drew a prize. They were praising her, she found, in terms sometimes extravagant, which pleased her none the less. But work and solitude began to tell upon her. She wanted to speak to some one. This feeling grew so strong that at last she determined upon an expedition. She would call upon her publisher.

It was a hot July morning, and she walked down Paternoster Row.

The firm of Pickering and Co. announces itself in letters of blazing gold, which he who runs may read; and without difficulty she found the house. She entered a sort of warehouse, where a clerk was writing at a desk, and asked if Mr. Pickering was disengaged.

"What name?" inquired the youth, shortly.

"Miss Chance."

His manner changed. Alighting from his high stool with alacrity, he requested Charity to "step this way, if you please," ushered her upstairs to a waiting-room, invited her to take a seat, and assured her Mr. Pickering would not be long.

She waited some minutes, and the time seemed endless. Mr. Pickering probably cherished no great desire to see her. She began to wonder at her temerity in calling, and to wish she had not come. Two large etchings adorned the wall, and she got up and stood looking at one of them. Then the door behind her opened. She turned round quickly, and was face to face with Alfred Prentice.

16

"Charity," he cried with rapture, just as when he met her unexpectedly in the wood. "How glad I am! I was going to write, and came here to-day to be sure of your address."

As he stepped towards her, she recoiled with aversion from his outstretched hand.

At once he stopped. His manner changed. But trouble had taught her much. A finer sense had replaced the freshness of her inexperience, and when he spoke again she could feel the vanity at work beneath his words.

"I wanted to congratulate you upon your book. It is fresh and sweet. A new note. Delicate, passionate, and shy, like the whisper of some woodland bird. Yet fierce in its relentless grip on an inevitable human destiny."

His voice sank into a whisper as he spoke of the bird he did not specify, and he clenched his fists and crushed the tragedy of all humanity between his set teeth.

Then he thought of himself, and became low and mellow as of old.

"But above all, I felt something due to

you, and still more to my own heart.
When we loved each other so madly, and
I would have carried you away," — he raised
his hands towards heaven to show how far
he would have carried her, — "the greatness
of your soul overcame me. You showed
me the crime I was committing, and the
inevitable consequence. I knew my weakness, and at least had strength of mind to
flee. Your story touched me deeply. I
saw your soul suffering the burden of another's wrong, and my heart melted with
pity. I could not write. Then, the sorrow
of my own poor life was thrown open to the
world. Ah! sad, sad! All is sad!"

Moved by the picture of his own magna-
nimity, he was quite overcome. His eyes
filled with tears. Unable to proceed, he
turned away and covered his face in his
hands.

The girl took one quick, impulsive step
towards him. Doubtless he loved her, whatever his misfortunes, and love demanded
sympathy at least. Then the recollection
of his coldness to her distress rushed into

her mind. He could never have loved her.
With sudden insight she perceived that this
man deceived himself, and had no stake in
human life. Imagination and he played
a game of chance, with mere words for
counters.

Recalled to himself by her movement, he
came towards her.

"Please do not speak to me, Mr. Prentice," she cried impatiently. "The past is
gone and better forgotten."

Her tone was so angry and contemptuous
that it hurt his pride, but the smart of the
injury completely restored him. He continued to explain himself.

"Then your book came into my hand.
Again I was about to write when I read of
the terrible affair at Babblemouth. I dared
not intrude upon your sorrow at such a
moment —"

"What do you mean?" she interrupted
him.

He looked at her in astonishment.

"Is it possible you have not heard of
Poltimore-Briggs?"

"I have heard nothing."

At once his manner became quite commonplace. He had no emotion to expend on a mere historical fact.

"He committed suicide by throwing himself over the cliff. The jury brought in an open verdict, but his affairs were in an awful state, and everybody knows what really happened. He had been living on the money of your little crippled friend for years. He was her trustee, and spent every penny or lost it in speculations. They thought he had run away. That yacht we sailed in was seized and sold. They found his body by the rocks where we lay becalmed after he had been gone a week."

"Mr. Pickering will see you now," said a voice beside her.

The clerk was standing by her elbow. She had not heard him come into the room. Like a person hypnotised and obeying a suggestion, she followed him along a passage, and was shown into an office. As she entered, a large man with red hair rose from his chair behind a table strewn with books and papers, and greeted her most cordially.

"How do you do, Miss Chance? I am most happy to make your acquaintance. You want to hear about your book. Well, I am glad to say it is going well, — fairly well. We 've pushed it in every way — advertised it heavily — almost too heavily, perhaps." Here he smiled benignly. "And it has been well reviewed. You would like to see some notices."

He laid upon the table before her a large volume into which press-cuttings had been pasted.

It should have been a moment of eager anxiety and triumph, but Charity could not read a word. Mr. Pickering was there as large as life. She saw him. She heard clearly every word he uttered, and she stared upon the open page. But she was not there at all. This was all a dream. The real Charity was far away at Babble-combe with poor Aunt Helen, deceived and penniless! What could become of her in such a situation?

Mr. Pickering stood rubbing his hands.

"And what are you doing now, Miss Chance?" he asked with friendly condescension.

There was a pause whilst the question pierced its way through her preoccupation. A minute later she remembered having heard it, and replied in haste, —

"I am finishing another book."

"We shall be very pleased, indeed, to see it, Miss Chance."

He nodded his head, and in smiling expectation awaited her reply.

But Charity did not answer. How could poor Aunt Helen support the want of those requirements which wealth had always provided? That was the thought which kept her dumb.

Such reticence on the part of a budding authoress was rare. A suspicion crossed the mind of Mr. Pickering that Charity must have been approached from elsewhere.

"Of course, Miss Chance," he explained in quite a lordly way, "we can do much better for you with a second book. We should increase the royalty *and* the advance. Of this I am quite sure, no one in the trade could do better for you than we."

Still no response. Nothing but a direct question could win a word from Charity.

"We might be able to run it in our magazine." He went on now very serious, and stroking his fat chin. "On consideration, I think we should like to look at what you have done at once. If it is suitable, and we give you, say, a hundred pounds for serial publication, and then—"

The girl looked up with disconcerting suddenness.

"How quickly could you let me know?" she asked.

"In the course of a day or so we would communicate our—"

She gave him no time to finish his sentence.

"I will fetch it at once and bring it to you. I hope there will be no delay. I am going into the country. I will give you my address."

She glanced at the table. He handed

her paper and a pencil, and she wrote: *C/o Miss Graham, Babblecombe House, Babblemouth.* Then before he could cross the room to open the door for her, she was flying down the stairs.

"Somebody has made that girl an offer," he muttered to himself. "I should really like to know how much they have said."

But Charity had only one thought, — to bring her precious manuscript and get to Babblecombe as quickly as she could. She looked for no train. She made no plan; but hurried thither and back, and at last must wait an hour upon the platform before she could depart.

She would return, and throw her arms around the little cripple's neck, without words or explanation, trusting only to the abiding power of their love. And she would keep her in poverty. And pay the debt of many years. And tend her as no hireling hands can ever tend.

It was evening when she reached the hilltop and once more looked down upon the

little mansion in the coombe. How quiet
it all was! Not a leaf of the ivy stirred.
There was no one in the garden, and Jan
Sprake was not in the yard.

She had brought nothing home, and above
the cottages she stopped the hired fly she
had taken at the station, and got out. She
would rather walk down unobserved.

The door was open, and she went in as if
she had but come back from the town. She
wandered across the hall and into the
drawing-room. The French window was
closed and fastened, and the place had the
close air and wore the dusty look of a room
not used.

A spirit of change and disaster brooded
everywhere. The things remained unal-
tered, but something had fled. No open
book lay upon the table, no paper had been
dropped in haste upon the floor. And the
chairs stood back against the wall, lacking
significance.

She heard a sound, — a man's step has-
tening out of the house. She ran back,
just in time to catch sight of the departing

figure of Bibberly, the bluff, fox-hunting, local practitioner, whom Miss Graham regarded with contempt bordering on abhorrence. Then Aunt Helen must be ill, — ill indeed to submit to his presence. How carefully he closed the door to make no noise!

She went upstairs and listened. She was afraid this suddenness of arrival might be ill-timed, and she did not know what to do. From the room where Miss Graham used to sleep came a low moan.

Charity stealthily opened the door and looked in. The little cripple lay upon a low chair beside the open window. The evening breeze bulged the white curtain and fanned her face. Her cheek was yellow like parchment, and bloodless like death. Yet her senses were alert, for the shrewd grey eyes, brighter than ever and very large, glanced round as the quickening current of air told her that some one was silently entering the room. At once they glistened with delight. She had gone too far upon the journey of life to feel surprise.

She tried to beckon with her finger as of old.

Charity ran to her.

"I was just thinking of you, child. Kiss me, Charity. Put your hair against my cheek. I knew you would come. Graham has been reading to me, Charity. Charity, you have it all, dear."

She quivered with excitement. In the intensity of her feeling her voice broke into a whisper.

The girl did not understand.

"Don't you remember what I once said? Soul, or passion, or a great heart. Graham has been reading to me — the book — my book — for I made you, child. He was sent for when the — when the trouble came, and he stays here for the present. He sat up with me last night. I made him go and lie down. I cannot sleep because of the pain, and the maid has run in for the draught. The Mortimers have gone to a garden-party to-day, and so I was alone. I was thinking of you. I knew you would come."

She paused, and gazed into Charity's eyes with such affection that the girl could not speak.

"It will be a very short time now, Charity," she said sadly. "I am quite ready, and have thought of everything. But I don't want to go. I want to stay — I want to stay more than ever."

Her thin hands firmly clutched the girl's shoulders, as though upon the secure stability of that young life her drifting spirit could anchor itself to earth. Then she became resigned.

"But everything is arranged, and my mind is at peace. The thought of John Sprake troubled me. For when the horses had to be sold, what was he to do? And he had been here twenty years, always faithful and safe. But what do you think, Charity? He has taken the George Hotel! I wrote to the justices about him. He has been really a wonderful man, so steady and saving. I can't think how he saved it all on fifteen shillings a week. But it was such a relief, child." One illusion at least had never been dispelled, and she smiled upon the girl as she went on. "Charity, there is the house and land, and seven hundred pounds in the bank that was not drawn out. That will keep you, just keep you, dear."

Suddenly she summoned all her energy. She raised herself in the chair. She spoke and pointed in the old way that Charity had never dared to disobey.

"Go and knock at Graham's door, child. Tell him to come at once."

Graham came in haste. He and the girl stood side by side, and through the window shone the last glow of the evening sun. It astonished Charity to see how greatly he was changed. A new ruddiness of travel was on his face. Trouble had hardened his will and given character to his features.

"What did you want, Aunt Helen?" he said tenderly.

Miss Graham looked at them, and the old desire came back. One last gleam of romance flashed from her departing soul, vivid as the momentary streak of flame that sets on fire a western cloud.

"Marry," she cried, — "marry at once. There will yet be time. And I shall see the wish of my heart."

He turned towards the girl in doubt. Even if she would marry him, could he dare to take advantage of the weakness of this moment?

"Marry!" repeated the little cripple, with wilder urgency.

The girl saw his hesitation. He was poor and unfortunate. The disgrace and death of his father must for ever overshadow him like a cloud. She could understand all that. Her heart went out towards him with a force of love it could never have known in the old summer days. She could comfort him, and help him, — yes, and earn money for him, too, if he would only ask her now. But the time was past. She also had lost an illusion. Nothing could bring back that.

As he looked, the light of love came into his eyes.

"Charity," he whispered quickly, "we have never broken it off."

"We have never broken it off," she echoed.

With a smile of satisfaction the little cripple sank back exhausted and said no more. She had got the wish of her heart, and that night she slept.

In the cold grey of early morning she passed away content.

They were married that summer in the little church beside the cliff looking down upon the quay, where Charity was left a waif. No one ever knew whence she came. They sold the little mansion, and left Babblemouth at once, and no one asked whither they went.

Her signature is on the register, and that is all.

That was the last of Charity Chance.